GHOST MOON

SHADOW LEGACIES

BOOK TWO

NAUGHTY NIGHTS PRESS LLC• CANADA

GHOST MOON

SHADOW LEGACIES SERIES,

BOOK TWO

COPYRIGHT © 2021

ERZABET BISHOP & GINA KINCADE

ISBN: 978-1-77357-477-6

978-1-77357-478-3

PUBLISHED BY NAUGHTY NIGHTS PRESS LLC

COVER ART BY WILLSIN ROWE

GHOST MOON

A ghost hunter. A demon cat. A grim history revealed.

Laurel Downing is in a bad spot. She needs to get her Nana out of an abysmal assisted living center, no ifs, ands, or buts about it. With the help of her demon cat, Thickety, she agrees to put her ghost-hunting mettle back to the test after a horrific accident nearly claims the life of her best friend. Ghosts are drawn to Laurel, and like her Nana says, with any great gift comes a great responsibility.

When Laurel agrees to take a job investigating the disappearance of a fellow ghost hunter at Greystone Asylum, she is totally unprepared for a sexy and stubborn psychic debunker to be a part of the package.

Gabe Parsons suffers no fool lightly—especially frauds who prey on the weak and grieving. A professional reality show host, he's seen his fair share of bad apples. One look at Laurel has him wondering just which side of the barrel she falls into. He knows there's something bad within the walls of Greystone Asylum. The voices of the past are alive behind the imposing iron gates. Now, he just has to prove it.

Can these two opposing forces, with the help of a very cranky demon cat, find the answers behind the asylum's crumbling walls before the asylum's grim history repeats itself?

DEDICATION

For my furry kids. You are my heart.

For my husband, who keeps me tethered in the now.

For Gina, who always makes me aspire to greater heights.

And for my friend Roseanne, who passed away this year from complications with Covid-19. I love you and miss you more than I can ever say.

PROLOGUE

"I KNOW HE'S here someplace. We just have to look." Zoe ducked under the collapsing doorway, vanishing from sight.

"Wait! What are you doing?" Laurel scurried behind her, her feet slipping on the debris-covered floor. "The foundation is ready to give. We shouldn't go in without backup."

"What backup?" Zoe called out, her

voice echoing in the hollowed out old place. "It's just us and your demonic cat. If we wait for backup, then the kid might not make it."

"What about Randall?"

"He's off chasing that orderly from Mercer House again. I haven't seen him in a week."

"Where's Lowell?"

"Off visiting his parents. Don't worry. We'll be fine."

Laurel groaned and stumbled into the crumbling front room. Barker House. Site of numerous murders and disappearances. It had loomed over the town for years, its ominous presence one Laurel hoped she never had to get near. It was bad enough the dead called to both her and Laurel. She didn't need a neon sign pointing at her. Ghost hunter—come eat me for lunch. Even with Thickety by her side, the place scared the holy mother crap out of her. And yet, here she was. Correction... here they were. She only hoped she didn't get them killed in the process.

Stupid. Stupid. Stupid.

But the life of a child was more important than her getting over her fear. It was bite the bullet time.

Zoe was always the one fighting her connection to the other side, so why was she so worried?

Something about this case scared the crap out of her, that's why.

What if it wasn't just a ghost causing all the trouble?

The dead, she could deal with, it was

the living that scared her.

Wallpaper hung in tattered sheets. Graffiti and litter were scattered around the decaying old furniture, evidence there had been someone staying here recently. She aimed the flashlight into the gloom.

"You better be right about this, Thickety."

No response.

"Figures. You head off to parts unknown just when I need you most. I hope you have fun while I'm—" Her foot snagged on something and she went down, collapsing hard onto her knees.

"Shit." Pain blossomed in her already sore legs and her knees sang songs of future bottles of ibuprofen. Laurel staggered to her feet, but not without first noticing the ghostly figure hovering in front of her. "Hello."

"You can see me." It wasn't a question. The woman was translucent, and judging from her clothes, had died recently.

"I can. How can I help you?"

"Ruby. My name is Ruby Watkins. But I'm here to help you." The ghost turned her face toward the stairwell. "He's up there. It's too late for me but you can help save my boy. The room at the top of the stairs on the right. But you have to hurry. He's got Alex behind the wall of the bedroom and he's going to seal the hole up tonight."

Sorrow, deep and abiding, emanated from the spirit, and Laurel had to consciously hold off the feeling before it invaded her. "Thank you, Ruby. Is he armed?"

The ghost shook her head. "No. He never needed to be. The man's dangerous all on his own. Just be careful. I miss my Alex, but I don't want him ending up the way I did. Stupid to trust that man. So stupid." Her face twisted into a mask of agony. "Just get him. Please."

"I will." Flashlight in hand, Laurel took the steps one at a time, knowing full well what could happen if the decayed wood gave way. She paused long enough to send a text message to her friend. Danny's father worked at the local police department. He'd come through before. But she didn't have time to wait to see if he got the text or not.

She swiped her phone closed and kept climbing.

Zoe had vanished into the gloom and she hadn't heard a thing. It was too silent, the only noise the creak of the stairs as she made her way up.

One foot after the other.

No games.

"Thickety, you are one skinned cat if you don't get your butt over here."

"What?" The demon cat appeared at the top of the stairs. He swished his tail, red eyes gleaming in the shadowy landing. "I'm watching the idiot in the next room and your very insane partner. She has a mallet. Whose brilliant idea was that?"

"Hers." Laurel took the last three steps and joined him on the second floor. "Is he in there?"

"Listen."

"The house wants you, Alex. It's always wanted a little boy to play with." The gibbering high-pitched male voice was met with the muffled sobs of a child.

"Let me out. Please. I want my mommy!" Alex wailed.

"Soon. You'll be with your mommy soon. Just a little more drywall paste to cover the wall and you'll be in there nice and secure. Then we wait. It only takes a few days. Then you'll be there with her for all time. And so will I."

The dark chortle at the end of the man's cryptic comments crept over Laurel's skin like a palpable thing. She grimaced and grabbed for her phone. Zoe had to be around here somewhere.

They both put their phones on vibrate whenever they went into a haunting. It was easier to talk without someone overhearing if there were any living people in the space like there was tonight.

Where are u?

"I'm here," came the whisper from across the hall. Zoe crouched in the shadows, mallet in hand. "Do you hear him?"

She didn't. Laurel had been so focused on finding Zoe, she forgot to worry about the psycho killer in the next room.

"Is there another way out?" She glared at Thickety, waiting for an answer.

"Yes. But he's still there. I can hear

two humans behind the wall. He's just finished sealing the drywall."

"Not for long." Zoe rose from her hiding spot and poked her nose around the corner. "Yep. Crazy bastard's gone and done it. The wall's sealed."

"I would recommend you not using that mallet." Thickety strolled forward and sniffed the wall. "This one is going to come crashing down on you, girl. Wait for the units to come. They'll just be pleased you found the boy. Now, let's go outside where it's safe?"

"We can't wait. If he's in there with that nut, there's no telling what he's doing."

Thickety leveled a glare at Laurel. "If you break down that wall, I won't be responsible for what happens. I just want you to understand that. There are other ways. Like waiting for the cops like you started to do."

Zoe shrugged and moved forward. "I appreciate it, Thickety, but we have to save him. I'll take the hit on this one. Something happens, it happens to me, deal?"

"Don't make a deal with a demon when you aren't prepared to lose, girl." Thickety narrowed his eyes in contempt. "You should know that by now."

The wall stood large and forbidding in front of them, silent save for the sound of their breathing. Then a cry resounded from behind the wood and drywall.

"To hell with that, demon." Zoe swung. The mallet broke into the wet drywall, shattering it onto the floor.

Swing after swing, the wall opened up and a gasping boy climbed out of the hole.

"Mommy! Where's my mommy!" He clung to Laurel and she held him as he sobbed.

"Hold onto me, Alex. Then you can see Mommy."

He lifted his grimy tear stained face and nodded.

"I'm here, baby." The ghost of Ruby Watkins wavered and came into view. "I'll always be with you. Now, you go with these ladies. I want you to be safe and get away from here."

"But mom..."

"No, sweetheart. I died. There's nothing more for me than to make sure you don't." The ghost leaned in and pressed her lips to her son's forehead. "This woman has the gift, and I'm thankful she found you. Now, go. He's still in there."

The ghost's words sent a chill down Laurel's back. "Zoe! Come on."

"I'm coming." She turned to leave the gaping maw in the wall. Sirens echoed in the distance and the flash of blue and red police lights flickered in the room.

"No. You're not." Garrison Connolly burst from the rubble, his head broken and bleeding. He grabbed at Zoe.

She swung, the mallet hitting another portion of the wall. "Get away from me!"

"I don't think so, chicky." He lunged at her, and she swung again, this time connecting. Connolly fell into the wall and, at the impact, the house trembled.

The wall she'd been beating on disintegrated, crashing down on Zoe and nearly burying her alive.

"Zoe!"

Oh, God. Lowell was going to kill her.

Connolly darted past her and directly into the waiting arms of Officer Chandler, her contact at the local police department.

"Going somewhere?" The click of cuffs and Connolly's cursing echoed down the hall as he was led away. Another female officer took charge of Alex. His mother watched from the sidelines, tears sliding silent down her face.

There was so much rubble. Laurel dug until it seemed like she'd never find her.

"Let me help you, Laurel." Irene

Chandler knelt down and started slinging debris.

"Thanks."

A limp, pale hand came into view.

"Zoe!"

"Hurry. She needs air or she'll suffocate." Officer Chandler plowed into the chunks of drywall, hurling the pieces out of their way.

Time seemed to stand still and all Laurel could hear was the breath moving in and out of her and the thud of the drywall hitting the ground. The dead moved in. She could feel them all around her, pressing too close. Wanting too much. If they had their way, Zoe would belong to them and that Laurel wouldn't have. Anger radiated from them, their energy coarse and brutal against the fragile state Laurel found herself in.

This was her best friend. The girl who'd stood up to her parents when she told them what she was going to do with her talent. Who believed in her when she held her hand and talked to a ghost for the first time on her own.

This was *Zoe*.

Then they found the rest of her. Laurel couldn't tell if she was breathing or not as they pulled her nearly lifeless body from the ruins of the wall. "Oh my God," Laurel whispered.

Thickety approached and lowered his head to Zoe's chest. "There is a heartbeat."

An acerbic retort came to her lips but she bit it back. Mouthing off to a demon cat wasn't going to help her friend. Not by a long shot.

Zoe had to be all right. She just had to. Vaguely, she heard someone come up beside her and the paramedics slipped into action. Adept at their work, they lifted her friend and placed her on a stretcher.

The emergency crew took Zoe away and with a pang, she realized this was all her fault. She should have stopped Zoe from heading off and doing something crazy.

Why hadn't she listened to Thickety?

Because she thought she knew better.

That was why.

As if reading her thoughts, Thickety turned his face away and it was then that Laurel saw the dozen or so ghosts lingering at the outskirts of the room.

These entities were hungry.

Feral.

She glanced into the eyes of one of the women who clutched at the hand of a young boy. She had lost much, but the hunger for revenge burned bright. The child turned his gaze to her and she couldn't help but look into his eyes. She moved forward and held out her hand without even realizing what she was doing.

"Laurel?"

The woman's smile twisted into something bordering on malicious delight. She took Laurel's hand and the flood of images came close to overwhelming her. Her breath came in shallow gasps. So much blood and pain.

It was a vortex of emotion and memories that built on itself as the specters crowded around her. It was too much.

She trembled and her body grew cold.

"Laurel. Step away," Thickety called out. He brushed against her legs, drawing her back into the physical realm.

Panic over what had just happened iced her blood. They had nearly taken her down with them just by touch. Zoe was her anchor. She held her hand and kept her tethered in the land of the living. The gray was just too strong. Laurel stumbled backward and almost fell as the glut of spirits followed.

Thickety roared, his true form emerging. The spirits cowered and shrank away. Laurel didn't have to think twice. She bounded to her feet and ran, leaving an openmouthed Officer Chandler in her wake.

CHAPTER ONE

LAUREL DOWNING QUIETLY let herself into the room where her grandmother lay nestled under the sheets, the blankets swallowing her slender frame. Nana needed her rest and was stubborn about admitting it. Laurel smiled at the sound of her steady breathing and light snoring. Pale and shrunken, she was a frail shadow of what she had been months ago. Peering over at her wizened face, she noted her grandmother's lips appeared chapped.

Damn it.

What do these people have against ChapStick?

It wasn't fair. Nana appeared to be shrinking right before her eyes. Laurel had already lost her parents. She didn't want to lose Nana, too. It was too much. Especially after everything they'd been through over the last year. Tears pricked at the corners of her eyes and she fought against them. She had to be strong.

No.

If Nana woke up and found her crying, there would be hell to pay. Laurel sniffled and forced her emotions in check. It was hard enough trying to finish high school, let alone pay the bills and try to be the adult when all she wanted to do was wake up from this nightmare. But no one was going to wake her. This was her new reality, like it or not.

"She needs to get out of here," Thickety blurted out, his shadowy form hidden in the dimness of the room. His long cat tail flicked his disdain, and he edged his head toward Laurel. Red eyes glowed from his smoky black form that could be as solid or transparent as he needed it to be. "The smell is worse than a cat box."

"Why do you keep following me? Can't you just leave well enough alone?" Laurel ground out, trying her hardest not to make eye contact with the demonic cat. He'd been in her life since she could remember and nowhere along the way had it ever been easy. "And I know that. Look at those bruises."

Laurel gave him a cold look but he only gave her the cat version of a shrug.

"Hey, I'm doing you a solid here. You want to know where the missing bracelet is that used to be on her arm? There you go."

"The last time I listened to you, someone almost died."

"Don't you mean ignore? I told you the child was in the house, not to go poking into foundation walls with no structure to hold them up. There's a difference, sweet cheeks." Thickety raised his paw and casually licked at his foot. "Remember, I was right. Just because your friend decided to get a little crazy with a mallet and found herself buried was *not* my fault."

Tears stung Laurel's eyes and she shoved them down. She wasn't going to think about it. Not now. Not when she had to go to work. If she dissolved into mush, it wasn't going to do her or anyone else any good. She sucked in a breath and grit her teeth. "Look. I came here to see my grandmother. Can we save the arguments for later?"

"Fine." The cat yawned and crept closer, his eyes focused on Laurel's Nana. "She used to be livelier than this. What are they feeding her?"

"I don't know but whatever it is, it's not enough. She looks terrible." Weak and more fragile than she had ever seen her. Laurel had to do something to get her out of here. Even if that something was take a job working for Harold Danvers. The past was the past. It was easy to say that until the nightmares came, leaving her shaking in her bed covered in sweat.

CHAPTER TWO

LAUREL DUG OUT the beaded, wooden bracelet her grandmother had given her for luck and massaged the beads between her fingers. She hadn't worn it since the accident, but it was time to put it back on. She was ready to try again. There was no other choice. People needed her. No part-time job in the world was going to pay for Nana's care. Even in this place and it was scraping the bottom of the barrel.

She turned to find Nana's eyes open, her cold blue gaze steady and considering. She never missed a trick. "How are you doing today, Nana?" Laurel perched on the edge of the plastic chair next to the bed, her hands knotted in her lap. The lamp on the nightstand was at its lowest setting. Perhaps Nana wouldn't notice the tears.

"No crying, *liebchen*." Her voice was soft, almost a rasp in the quiet room. Her frail hand shook as she reached out to her granddaughter. "I see the cat is here as well."

"Nice to see you, too." Thickety doffed his head and approached the bed, sitting down a respectable distance away.

Laurel took her grandmother's hand

in her own, taking note of the bruises that covered her arms where the nightgown didn't conceal them. In the shadows of the room, the mottled colors looked black. Anger coursed through her as she considered how they came to be there. "What is this, Nana?"

"I hit my arm on the wall." Nana struggled to sit up, pressing the remote control button on the bed, easing her into a sitting position. "There. That's better."

Noises filtered through the door and a scream from an enraged elderly resident could be heard through the wall next door.

"Funny how many walls seem to have it in for you these days."

"*Liebchen.*" A stern look passed

between them.

Laurel sighed. "I know. I know." She scooted the chair closer. "I have a new job that might help me get you out of here."

Her grandmother considered her for a moment. "Are you ready to try again?"

"She has to." Thickety responded as if the question were aimed at him. "If she doesn't, she'll always be afraid."

Laurel rolled her eyes at the cat. "So dramatic. As much as I hate to admit it, he's right. There isn't much of a choice. Either I take the job, or work nights in the spaghetti factory down the street after my day job at the store." Laurel's voice was firm. "I have to. For you."

Her grandmother exhaled. "Do what you need to do for *you*. I'll be fine." Her wrinkled face pulled together in a frown. "I don't want to be a burden."

"You aren't." Laurel snorted. "This place is killing you. If I could take you home this minute, I would."

Nana smiled. "I don't suppose I'd want to climb all those stairs right now, precious girl. Perhaps tomorrow."

Laurel laughed. "Okay. Tomorrow. We'll get you fitted with some track shoes and I'll find a foldout bed that fits in the kitchen. What do you say? We can kick Thickety out. He doesn't eat anyway."

The cat made a noise of disgust. "You two are terrible. If I knew where to find your spirit guide, I'd drag his sorry backside here just so he has to endure the same torment I do."

Nana narrowed her eyes in irritation. "If you do that, Thickety Ironskin, I will get out of this bed and find the first bottle of salt I can get my hands on and cast your demon backside back to the fires of Hell. If I wanted Jasper, I would call him. I won't have him bound here. Not after all he had to endure for my sake."

"Nana..." Laurel didn't know what to say. All the women in their family had contact with the gray world in one way or another.

Except her mother.

And she punished you for it every day of her life, too.

"Do we understand each other, demon?"

Thickety stretched to his feet and

flicked his tail. *"Fine.* You don't have to get your knickers in a twist about it. I was merely making a suggestion. It might help if you had some protection in this place. If Jasper knew where you were, he'd be honored to help. He speaks of you often."

"I don't want to hear another word about it. If I summon him here, he'll be trapped by my side, and I won't have it. Not again." Nana's tired eyes snapped in the dim room and she turned to Laurel. "Now, tell me about this job."

"Do you remember a place down on Highway One called Greystone Asylum?" Laurel leaned back in the chair, preparing for one of her grandmother's endless stories. She had one for nearly every occasion, and it never failed to put

Laurel at ease. That was what she needed right now.

After the terrible way her last venture into the gray world had gone, she'd hung up her ghost-hunting heels in favor of more menial tasks. The look on her best friend's face when the decrepit wall of the house they were investigating came crashing down on top of her was forever burned into her brain. It didn't matter that Thickety had tried to help. It had gone to hell so quickly there was nothing anyone could do.

At the horrified gasp that erupted from Nana's lips, Laurel sat up. "Harold Danvers is thinking about turning it into an amusement park for hobbyist ghost hunters. He wants me to go and check it out to see if there's anything to the legends or if it's just bunk."

"No," her Nana whispered, her face growing even more pale. "Not there. Never there, my *Liebchen*."

"What's wrong?" Laurel reached out to touch her, but her grandmother flinched. "It's been abandoned for years."

The old woman curled into herself on the bed, staring far into the distance. She sucked in a half sob and moaned, a terrible sound that chilled Laurel to the bone. "That place," she hissed. "So many horrors. So many."

Laurel's heart beat faster in her chest. "What do you mean? You've seen it?"

"I've been there." Dry laughter, brittle and raspy, rattled out of Nana's lips. Her eyes opened and glittered in the half-light. The haunted mien was still present, but she spoke. "Your great-grandparents, in their fear, institutionalized me when I wouldn't stop talking about the strange people hiding in the shadows. That and a certain cat would come and visit me, and I didn't understand."

"What do you mean?"

"You have your Thickety, but you know when to talk to him and when it is best to be silent, no?"

Laurel nodded.

"A hard lesson, too," The cat groused.

"It was very difficult for Jasper and I." Her rheumy eyes swam with water and painful memories. "In those days, they confined young women for anything. You didn't do what people wanted or cow down to their social mores, they locked you away for rehabilitation."

"Rehabilitation?"

"Yes. Parents unable to control their children often sent them someplace where they didn't have to deal with them. People who, in society's eyes, defied the laws of nature. Women who would not bend to their husbands' will. All of it. All of them. So many innocents locked away for the crime of wanting to be nothing more than themselves." Her grandmother's voice was tinged with bitterness.

Laurel met her grandmother's eyes with trepidation.

Had Jasper's presence been what sent her away?

Laurel had first encountered Thickety

when she was a small girl, but her mother had never seen him. Either that or she never wanted to.

"Then there are those of us who see beyond the veil. That makes the rest of the world more than a little uncomfortable."

"Like Mom. And Zoe."

Just whispering her name sent a stab of guilt through her. She missed her friend.

"Yes, my dear. Like your mother."

"How did your parents find out about Jasper?"

Nana looked off into space. "It was the shadow people from the gray who found me first. They frightened me. I was only a child the first time."

"So your mother never saw them?"

"No. As we've found out, it can skip generations."

"I had you. The first time they came to me in the night. I called you and Jasper brought Thickety."

"He did, too." The cat sat proud, his tail twitching. "You were a sniveling little thing."

She had been. Crying and shaken, she'd called down the hall to her grandmother and she'd come, no questions asked. It had been months later when she realized no one but she and her grandmother saw the ghosts. Other people didn't have spirit guides and that made her feel even more like a freak than she already was.

Her parents didn't like the influence her grandmother had over her and they moved away, sending Nana off on her own and Laurel to a place very much like Greystone, only more modern. More antiseptic. The strong scent of bleach always brought the experience sailing back like a bad dream. It had only been for two weeks but they had been the longest two weeks of her life. From then on, she'd always been the crazy one.

Until Zoe.

The dead crowded around. She hated this place with its reek of ammonia and bleach and the perpetual stream of restless spirits that sought her aid. Laurel clutched the beads in her hands and gave them all a mental push back.

How did her grandmother stand it here?

Nana's intelligent dark gaze watched

her. "I see them, too." She lifted a fragile, gnarled hand and captured one of Laurel's in her own.

"You're not crazy, *Liebchen*. The world just doesn't want to accept things it can't see." She paused and pointed to the beads in Laurel's hand. "What you don't see *can* hurt you—you realize that now, don't you?" A sad smile touched her lips and the distant expression crept back in.

"She better." Thickety growled. "Stupid girl almost died herself. Let alone her friend."

"I know," Laurel whispered. Leaving the abandoned house filled with homicidal ghosts was an awful thing and not something she was proud of. But she had to get her strength back before she tackled them again. Her confidence. That was part of what she was hoping for with Greystone. But as she sat there, a realization hit her.

If one house could hold so many malevolent spirits, what would an asylum have buried within its walls?

The thought made her shiver. She would need more than Thickety to make it out of there alive.

"Is that how you do it? Not see?"

But there wasn't an answer.

How could there be?

They each had to do what they needed to do block out the visions and the voices.

Thickety was her salvation and her curse. There was no in between. He could ground her temporarily but she needed Zoe. Or at least another person in her stead.

She had to get her Nana out of here. Like it or not, she was going to have to pull on her big girl panties and get herself together. Everything was at stake and she couldn't afford to be afraid.

She'd visited Zoe in the hospital and there had been no change. Such a near brush with death had to have its consequences and Laurel wanted to be there for her when she woke. She hated hospitals as much as nursing homes but there was no other choice. With every trip, she got a little bit stronger. The nurses had her number and she checked in with them almost every day. Being without her right arm felt so unnatural and being brave without her was a hollow endeavor at best.

"I have no choice but to see, my girl. I just choose not to look. Not anymore."

"But Greystone..."

"Is a terrible place. One that will suck you in and never let you out. I was lucky... so lucky to escape." Her grandmother's brow wrinkled in concentration and then her eyes closed.

Nana closed back in on herself and the shivering began in earnest. Where she went, Laurel couldn't follow. The past had too many ghosts, and she was powerless to help. Nana rocked, curling into a ball, humming an unfamiliar tune. She wanted to protect her but she didn't know how.

The myriad gathering of spirits pushed at her, clawing at her essence.

They were like vultures picking over the dead and dying, taking bits and pieces of Nana slowly in her weakened state.

"Nana..." But there was no answer save for the broken tune spilling from her paper-thin lips.

Laurel had to push them back. "Thickety. Help me." She kept one hand on her grandmother and with the other she reached out to touch the demon.

"What do you want me to do?" He curled his tail and flicked it. "She needs Jasper. These entities are going to drain her if we let them remain. I can't try to block you both."

"It's a nursing home. The place is full of ghosts. Besides, if you do that, she'll never forgive you."

The cat gave her a scornful glare.

"That, my dear human, is a chance I'm willing to take."

Laurel considered his words. "Do it then. I have to try and reach her."

She held on tight to the wooden bracelet and tried to ease herself into the place where the spirits of the past spoke, at the same time keeping the restless dead around her at bay. With Thickety as a support, it was easier to control them. She couldn't even imagine what her Nana had to contend with on a daily basis without her Jasper. Here, in this place, it was a foolhardy thing to do, but if she kept in contact with Nana she might be capable of helping her without getting sucked in. As long as Thickety didn't go too far that is.

"Can you call him from here?"

"I can."

"Go ahead. She can blame me when she wakes up."

Laurel reached out and touched her grandmother's shoulder, holding on for dear life. Hers and her grandmother's. She had never done this before, but maybe... just maybe, she could do it. It worked with the spirits and she prayed with all she was worth she might find the strength to do it now.

Laurel closed her eyes and reached out with that part of her mind she and her grandmother shared.

The otherness.

Visions of shadows came into view. Places her Nana had been. Glimpses of her past flooded in, paired with the emotions they invoked. It came at her in a rush of images and sensations that left her gasping for air.

Then something severed the connection, sending Laurel backpedaling back into herself. The force of it slammed her against the chair and toppled her to the floor. The beads flew from her hand and landed underneath the bed.

"Damn it!" Laurel scrabbled on her hands and knees, reaching beneath the hospital bed for the wooden beads. Nothing. With a shudder she laid her head on the floor and spied them inches away from where she lay. Laurel grasped them in her hand. She sprang up and dove for the chair.

That force, whatever it was, would not keep her from her task. Shaken, she reached out and touched her grandmother's shoulder once more.

It hunkered there, waiting. This time she recognized it for what it was.

Terror.

Her grandmother was blocking *her*.

"No! Nana, it's me. It's Laurel. I'm trying to help you." Fierce and determined, Laurel gritted her teeth and pressed inward.

The images locked behind the force remained clouded with age. Long hallways and darkened rooms. The sound of crying and the incessant movement of rocking. Always rocking and that damned song, it stuck there. A child's song about ashes and falling down. The sensation of being struck. The white caps of nurses and the belligerent orderlies pushing her into a darkened room. Solitary. Another place. Deep down inside the belly of the beast. A kindly face that held the soul of a monster.

Her grandmother screamed and thrashed, breaking the connection. *"No! Oh God, no!"*

"Nana?" Panic roiled through her. *"Tell me!"* Laurel scrambled up out of the chair and pulled the covers over her. She brushed a long strand of white hair out of her face, tucking it behind her ear, praying she would open her eyes one last time before she had to leave.

"What is it? Please!"

With great effort, her grandmother opened her eyes and turned her embattled gaze to meet Laurel's "Stay away. Far, far away," she gasped, clawing at her throat. "Terrible. So many..."

"Laurel, stop. It's too much." Thickety weaved on his feet, his small body weakened by the effort of keeping both women safe.

"Nana! I'll call the nurse." She raised her finger toward the button on the side of the bed but her grandmother closed her hand around her wrist in a vice grip.

"Laurel..." she gasped and her eyes rolled backward, her head sinking against the pillow. She shuddered and went still.

Laurel pressed the panic button on the bed and choked back a scream. "Oh God. Nana!"

Three nurses pushed their way into

the room, intent on their patient.

Jasper emerged from the shadows of the room, giving Laurel a baleful glance. The orange marmalade cat's eyes sparked red with irritation. "Thank you for bringing me back into service but I wish you'd let her be. If you must go, be careful Laurel Downing. And remember, the past and the present aren't that different after all."

"I'm sorry, Miss, but you must wait outside."

She started to speak to Jasper, but only nodded. Relieved he was there to watch over her while she was gone, she let herself be herded out the door.

"Nana," she whispered and pressed her hand to the door. "Please, hold on."

CHAPTER THREE

GABE PARSONS SIGHED in disgust. "That's a wrap, Frank." He signaled to his camera crew and propelled himself toward the front door.

Another supposed haunting.

Another con woman rooking a good family out of hard-earned money during a period of grief and unrest.

Anger raced through his veins at the audacity of the woman at the root of it all. Every single thing he found was explained by science. Rattling pipes and smoke and mirrors provided by the supposed ghost hunter. It made him positively ill.

"Mr. Parsons. You owe me another chance," came the biting voice from the farmhouse dining room. Wilhelmina Pruitt stalked toward him, spitting mad. The Goth getup she wore made her appear even more ridiculous than she already did. Powdered white makeup with black lipstick looked good if you had the air to pull it off. The woman in front of him didn't. Not by a long shot.

Ghost hunter, my ass.

"No. I don't think so. The family you tried to *help* called me out here for a reason." He snapped his notebook shut and pushed past her, intent on the door.

"Yeah? What reason is that? You and I are the same, Parsons. We both have a line to sell. Don't you ever forget it. Ghosts are real. You see them your way and I see them mine." She tried to insert herself in front of the door, but he brushed her aside with no more effect on him than a gnat.

"I don't expect you'll be seeing more than a suspended business license when the report goes live. You pinned a family's misfortune on their daughter's puberty? Really, Ms. Pruitt? Do we want to talk about the smoke machine and the mirrors I found set up in the attic? Or how about the dead crow nailed to the front door?"

The woman stared at him in hostile

disbelief, the angry fire in her eyes crackling.

"I didn't think so." Gabe left her standing there and walked out into the chilly autumn night.

***

Gabe cracked open a beer and sat down at his desk. The two monitors he had set up were ready and rolling footage from the night's adventure.

He hated people who took advantage of folks' fears and insecurities. He saw what it had done to his mother. The empty hooks and dangling promises never realized. Not until the money was gone and so were they.

When he was old enough, he'd found the woman who marked his mother for a fool and a rube and took her down first. As far as he knew, she was still doing time in the federal penitentiary for fraud. She could stay there and rot for all he cared.

He processed the key pieces of evidence and got it ready to send the lot over to his buddies at county. They would follow up on the investigation and find out if the amazing Ms. Pruitt had any other outstanding warrants.

God, he hoped so.

These frauds were like roaches. You see one and you know there's more beneath the surface waiting to be exterminated. And damned if he didn't love his job. So did the television station that'd picked up the show.

In this era of ghost hunting

programs, his was markedly different. It exposed the fakers for what they really were. The public loved it. He thanked his lucky stars every day and toasted Professor Lumley at the science center at Newsome College for his persistent meddling in his education. Hell, his double masters in communications and physics had to count for something.

Switching over to e-mail, he double checked his inbox and paused. A name he hadn't seen in a good long time sat looking back at him.

Harold Danvers.

It had been a few years but he'd never forgotten the association he had with the name. His contemporary Misty Duncan had taken a job to check out Greystone Asylum. At the time, Danvers wanted to make it into a fun park. When Misty told him about the plan, he laughed and told her it would never fly. The place was unsafe at best and probably riddled with homeless and drug addicts now that it was abandoned.

She went in but she never came out. Danvers had been beside himself. Gabe had been out of state on another case, but the man had tracked him down via the station.

He wanted to know if Gabe could look into Misty's background and see if there was anything or anyone who would want her dead. He hadn't been able to find a thing. Even a trip canvassing the lonely grounds of the asylum estate had left him with nothing.

If he had a hunch, he would have

thought maybe a run in with a homeless person. After that debacle, the project must have fizzled.

Now here Danvers was again.

He clicked on the e-mail and began to read.

"Well, I'll be damned." He was going back to the original project. To turn the property into an amusement park. The ghost hunters were going to have a fit. Greystone was one of the top haunted locales on the east coast.

The question was, why did Danvers want him there after all this time?

He hadn't been able to find any information about Misty's disappearance then.

What made him think it would be any better now?

The invitation was for a ten o'clock meeting. He toyed with the bottle of beer and took a swig of the dark German brew.

Go or not?

His calendar was empty for a couple of days while he wound up his latest project.

Why not?

In any event, he'd always wanted another crack at Greystone. He owed Misty. There were far too many secrets buried within its walls and Parsons itched to have the chance for another opportunity.

CHAPTER FOUR

"OH, COME ON!" Laurel pleaded as the elevator car lurched upward and shuddered to a stop, leaving her stomach somewhere between the floors.

Nauseous, she moved down the carpeted hallway toward the conference room door, trying to make her knees cooperate. She'd arrived early. Thank God. To be late for an appointment with Harold Danvers would be tantamount to kissing the contract good-bye. Already on edge from the visit with her grandmother last night, she was at least thankful traffic had cooperated for once.

With the close to single digits in her checking account, there was no way in hell she would do anything to mess up her chances on this case.

She tore her thoughts from her grandmother and gazed through the conference room doors, her gaze landing on her new boss. Well dressed in a dark brown suit, Harold Danvers possessed a casual elegance most men never achieved. She liked the man. He seemed honest and he wanted to hire her to investigate whether the strange goings on at Greystone Asylum were a real haunting or just wishful thinking on his part.

Laurel stared hard into the conference room. Danvers wasn't alone. Her new boss stood with his back to her and leaned against one of the conference room chairs. He was talking with none other than Satan himself.

Gabe Parsons.

Dark tendrils of hair curled across Gabe's broad forehead. Massive shoulders more than filled out the gray suit and dark blue dress shirt he sported. The gray and silver tie stressed the dazzling blue of his gaze. His stance emphasized the muscular nature of his thighs and the slimness of his hips. Despite herself, she found her gaze locking on his full lips and the devilish look in his eyes. Dangerously attractive, the man oozed sex appeal.

Yep.

Eye candy all the way.

It was a shame he had to be such a prick.

Host of the ever-popular cable show *Debunk This,* he spent his entire career making a mockery of psychic investigators.

Why the hell had Danvers invited him?

It made little sense.

Didn't he have faith in her abilities?

He had tracked *her* down, not the other way around.

Anger sizzled along her spine and she let it drive her on. Something had to. If she got lost in worrying about Nana or her power to keep the ghosts under control, it was all over. Deep down, she knew it was irrational, but the fear still reared up when she recalled the final moments of discovering who had been behind the murders of all the children and the residual phantasmal overflow that still remained.

Stop it.

Focus.

"Well, crap." Laurel smoothed down her skirt and sucked in her stomach. Using the glass to her advantage, she tucked a mutinous strand of blonde hair behind her ear and sighed. She looked the part in her tailored suit. Navy blue, with an ivory shell. Pearls and black heels. Tasteful. Practical. Ready to take on the doubting jackass in the next room.

Mostly.

She *was* capable. It had been three months, and she needed the work. The alternative wasn't worth bothering about. Laurel let out a heavy sigh and took a step forward. She could do this. She said a quick prayer under her breath, touching her grandmother's wooden bracelet tucked inside the suit's tiny pocket. With every movement, she felt it brush against her body and it bolstered her courage.

She would be who her grandmother expected her to be.

Who *she* needed to be.

Who she had been before her world had come spiraling to an end.

She missed Zoe. The accident had robbed her of more than just a coworker, but a friend. She was still rehabilitating at home with her family.

The broken bones were only the beginning. The other horrors of that night had to be scrubbed out of both their minds with an industrial-sized Brillo pad and a good dose of tequila.

"You'll do fine. Just get the job." Thickety moved beside her, his steadying presence keeping her from running back to the elevator.

Why was Parsons here?

Didn't Danvers trust her?

Laurel pushed open the door and strode inside. If Mr. Danvers wanted a ghost hunter to test out his property, she would do her job.

To hell with Parsons.

And his gorgeous eyes.

Don't stare.

"Mr. Danvers. How nice to see you." She turned her head and nodded toward the television personality and tried not to show any reaction. "Parsons."

Yep.

Still had that sexy cleft in his chin.

She had memorized it after hours of watching him tear down hardworking investigators. There may have been one or two she wondered about, but she couldn't believe every single one of the people on his show were the frauds he made them out to be. Parsons was even more gorgeous in person, and she cursed her wonky libido for noticing.

"Thanks for coming by, Laurel." Danvers smiled, extending his hand to clasp hers in greeting. "We were just discussing some of the pros and cons of the new project."

"Ms. Downing. How nice to meet you." Parsons's eyebrows rose and his gaze leaped to Danvers. The superior way he looked down on her set her teeth on edge.

"The pleasure is all mine." Laurel took a deep breath and adjusted her face to what she knew would be a winning smile. She held out her hand in a defiant gesture and shook Parsons's without looking at him.

What was her new boss up to?

Parsons didn't appear to be aware she'd been invited to the meeting any more than she'd known about him.

So what was going on?

"Danvers here tells me you're a ghost

hunter of sorts."

"Of sorts?"

"Yes, my dear. All of us are so very sorry to hear about your partner. Is she doing better?"

"She is, but the progress is slow."

"I'm sorry to hear that." Parsons nodded, his face unreadable. "Have you been on any cases lately?"

Ah.

Testing the waters to see if he can find a trail to follow.

Irritation and physical attraction scrabbled for dominance in her lower belly. "Not since the accident. No."

"Well, it's about time to get back in the saddle then." Danvers smiled and patted her arm. "I look forward to what you can tell me about the project and your reaction to the team I'm putting together."

Team?

Laurel considered Parsons. His haughty expression must have been mirrored her own to some degree. "Do you work with a team generally, Mr. Parsons?"

"Have you seen my show?"

"I have." She smiled, certain it didn't meet her eyes.

Every damned episode, you pompous Neanderthal.

Just bash it on the head if you don't understand.

As long as you look hot in a pair of khaki slacks and some rugged outdoorsman clothes, no one will mess with your ratings.

Laurel beat back her snarky inner voice and plastered a cream cheese smile on her face. Politics and getting paid.

Remember Nana.

This is for Nana.

Then you can walk away and never see him again.

"The camera crew and the boys who work on the footage for the station make up most of the team."

"So, you just prod? Is that it?"

The perfectly chiseled jaw tightened into a tight-lipped smile. "You could say that."

"I thought so."

"Now, now. Let's play nice. We want Laurel's first case after her absence to be smooth sailing. Let's save the banter for after we get started, shall we?"

"Now that I think of it, I do believe I did hear a thing or two about the accident. What a shame," Parsons replied, his eyes glittering in the subdued light of the office.

Was he fucking mocking her?

Oh hell no.

"How fortunate I haven't been asked to be on one of your episodes." She heard how stiff and unnatural her voice sounded, but didn't give a damn. She was here for Danvers and the job, not to assuage his obviously overblown male ego.

Laurel smiled, turning to Danvers. "You wanted to meet to talk about the potential for hauntings on the property?" She slid two sets of documents from her briefcase. She handed one to Danvers and after a moment, passed the other one to Parsons. "You're welcome to have mine. I didn't realize there would be three of us."

Thickety shot her a warning gaze. "A little bitchy there, don't you think?"

She pointedly ignored him, focusing instead on the people in the room.

"There will be one more person in attendance." Danvers cleared his throat and smoothed back a strand of gray hair. He stepped away from Laurel and walked to the window, leaving her and Parsons staring after him. The older man turned, facing them both, an expression of apprehension on his weathered face.

"I have a few concerns over whether the locale will have sufficient paranormal activity to host the haunted attraction I have in mind. Laurel, that's where you come in. Your primary work has been in finding missing persons and ferreting out the root cause of hauntings. I need your expertise in this matter."

He cleared his throat, glancing at Parsons. "You are reputed for debunking psychic claims and getting down to brass tacks. Your determination and circumspect appraisal is imperative before we can move forward. As a side note, I appreciated your work a few years ago and I'm hoping you can perhaps shed some new light on an old topic."

"Why do my findings matter when you've already decided to buy the place?" Parsons inquired, his eyes pensive.

Danvers inclined his head. "Excellent question. Give me a few moments and I'll be able to answer it more effectively."

"Sir, the document on the asylum will give you some case history." Laurel tilted her lips in a smile. This wouldn't be so bad after all.

They were all after the same goal, weren't they?

Maybe she wouldn't have to kill him. All he had to do was stay out of her way and everything would be fine.

"No need, Laurel. I've learned more about that asylum than I ever wanted to know."

"Sir?"

He doesn't want documentation on the hauntings?

"Bear with me. Our last party should arrive in a moment." Danvers poured himself a glass of water from a pitcher.

"Would you two care for a glass?"

"No, thank you," Gabe responded.

"Yes, please." Laurel accepted the glass Danvers poured out for her.

All eyes focused on the conference room door. Her grandmother's fear swam behind her eyes and she had to bite down on her lip to keep from reacting. Everything was at stake. If Danvers wanted her to dress like a Martian and wear a bikini she would do that, too. She had to get Nana out of that place as soon as possible.

Thickety brushed up against her leg from beneath the table.

Motion through the glass door caught her eye. The elevator doors slid apart and a man stepped out, striding with purpose toward the conference room, papers in hand. Barely stopping for the closed door, he pushed it open and walked toward the group.

"Harold. Here are the papers you were waiting for. Sorry I took longer than I intended." Warm brown eyes moved over her, lingering on her longer than was necessary.

"Laurel, Gabe. This is Saul James. He is my assistant and will act on my behalf in the acquisition of Greystone Asylum." Danvers smiled at the new arrival. "I'm glad you made it. We need to get started."

"Very nice to meet you." Laurel held out her hand in greeting. When he didn't release it, her eyes narrowed in speculation.

Thickety hissed, his red eyes glowing

with intent to do harm. Laurel gave him a slight shake of her head as a signal not to get involved—yet.

"Mr. James—" Laurel protested. Danvers was looking at the papers Saul had given him and was in another world. Laurel's startled gaze met Parsons's in a silent plea. She struggled to pull her hand out of Saul's steady grip.

"Good to meet you. Gabe Parsons." Parsons held out his hand and stepped between them.

Saul frowned, but smoothed his features over once again as he released Laurel and shook the other man's hand.

Laurel ran her hand over her skirt and took a step toward Parsons. Perhaps there was hope for him yet. Laurel gave him a considering appraisal. There was more than met the eye here. That meant she needed to keep her wits about her. There was too much at stake. Her fingers sought the wooden bracelet secreted away inside her pocket, and she relaxed.

"Let's get started. Why don't you have a seat? There is something I want to discuss with all of you."

"Good. Why don't we all sit down then?" Saul motioned to the conference table.

Now that's weird.

I thought Danvers was running the meeting.

Laurel sank into a chair, her gaze brushing over Parsons's. She wasn't sure how this was all going to roll, but one thing was sure, she would enjoy figuring it out.

CHAPTER FIVE

GABE SAT DOWN, still watching the enigmatic Ms. Downing. He'd loosely followed her career in psychic investigation. If he remembered correctly, she'd helped in several cases of lost children and one woman murdered by her husband.

The last case she'd worked on hadn't gone so well for her. A friend had been injured and this was the first job she'd taken since.

What had driven her out of her forced retirement?

It was clear she had understood she was the only one on the case. So had he. He still had doubts whether she was the real deal or just a great looking set of legs in a skirt.

So why the subterfuge on Danvers's part?

It didn't make a whole lot of sense.

Her almost brittle mannerisms indicated she viewed him as a threat and the realization hit that she figured he was here to prove her a fraud. Considering the tone of most of his episodes, he applauded her for her astute perception. He didn't suffer fools, or leeches out to make money on other people's misfortune. Maybe Danvers was using him for that purpose. It would spice up the publicity once the park opened. If it opened, that is. It didn't matter to him as long as he got paid.

He had initially come to find out what Danvers was up to with the old asylum. He wasn't at all convinced his last expedition ended like his assistant said it did. Laurel being here was even more incentive to stay. Proving another fake trying to make a buck on a friend's death would make his day. In fact, he was counting on it. Misty Duncan had been an admired colleague, and to die at Greystone was a travesty.

What other conclusion could he make?

Gabe took in the shapely Ms.

Downing. The conservative blue suit hugged her figure in all the right ways, and as she leaned in to take a sheet of paper from a stack of reports, he scented the faint aroma of her perfume.

Saul went to a side table and picked up some folders. He slid them in front of each person, himself taking a chair next to Danvers.

"I am looking to purchase Greystone Asylum." Danvers sat back in his chair, his gaze meeting Laurel's across the table "My reasons are my own, but you deserve to know of what you're walking into if you take the job." He picked up a pen and dropped it on a legal pad in front of him, making a point to glance in Gabe's direction.

"Three years ago, I hired a psychic

investigator to check out the asylum for traces of psychic energy and paranormal activity. You are familiar with the name Misty Duncan?"

Laurel nodded, her lips twisting into a frown. "She vanished a few years ago on a job."

Folding his hands in front of him, Gabe leaned forward. "We were colleagues. I never understood what happened. Even after walking the grounds." He met Danvers's gaze.

"Wait. She disappeared on your project?" Laurel said, surprised.

"Yes." Harold Danvers glanced down at the table, his lips a thin line of disapproval. "She was the original choice to vet the asylum and give me a report on the viability of having real psychic phenomena encapsulated in the entertainment factor. I hired her as a solo operator, with Saul as my presence in the investigation. She went in... and, well, she didn't come out." He sat back, the springs in the chair squeaking as he settled.

"They never found her. Not her body or any evidence of what went on there," Gabe murmured. "You kept it out of the press."

"That's correct."

"Why would she go into the asylum alone?" Laurel wondered aloud. "That's suicide. The grounds are a network of tunnels and buildings. God. You might get lost in there and never find your way out."

"She wasn't," Saul interjected. "I went

in with her."

"Then perhaps you can shed light on what happened. Women don't just vanish into thin air." Gabe's voice was flat, moving toward hostile. He had his suspicions from his investigation into Misty's disappearance. Nothing was ever found. Something was off here, and he was going find out what it was.

Danvers ignored the bickering, focusing his gaze on Gabe and Laurel. "I want you to go back to Greystone and do what Misty should have been able to do. Find out if the site is a viable investment for my amusement park. In the paperwork there, you'll find a tentative mockup of the plans for the estate, should we choose to invest.

"Gabe, you have the investigative

mind of a skeptic. I want you to go in there and find out what you can about what happened." He turned to Laurel. "You have a gift for reaching out to the dead. If Misty is there, I want you to find her. If there is any activity, I want to be appraised of the smallest detail."

"But..." Laurel sputtered. "So, she died, then? Is that what you're saying?"

With every word, Gabe observed Saul's flushed face. He was obviously having some difficulty with his boss's decision to go back into the asylum.

I wonder why that is...

Danvers's expression shuttered and he closed his eyes. Jaw clenched, he opened them again. "Yes. I believe that's what happened."

Saul threw down his packet of

papers, shaking his head vehemently. "We don't know that." His gaze moved over Laurel. "I couldn't find her. We got separated and that was it. The place is like a rabbit warren."

"That doesn't explain what happened," Laurel stated.

"I don't have to *explain* anything." Saul's eyes bored into Parsons and cut a path toward Laurel. His face was red and his eyes narrowed into slits. "You weren't there. I was. End of story."

Gabe watched as Laurel's expression closed in on itself. "Somehow I doubt that."

"I'm not discussing this. It's ancient history. We're here for a purpose, not to rehash the past." A vein throbbed in Saul's neck.

But we are, Saul.

What don't you want us to find?

"The dead tell no lies, do they, Ms. Downing?"

"No." Laurel sent Parsons a perplexed look. "They don't."

"That's exactly my point." Gabe stood. "I'll take your offer, Danvers. When do you want to begin?"

Laurel pushed up from the table.

"I accept it as well."

"Excellent." Danvers rose. "We'll start first thing in the morning. Everyone will meet outside the gates at six thirty." He paused. "There's one more thing."

"What's that?"

"Saul is going in with you."

Gabe walked out of the conference room, following close behind Laurel. She was in a hurry to leave and he couldn't blame her. Being in Saul's presence was like standing next to an oil slick. The man gave him the creeps. He dug his keys out of the pocket of his slacks and hit the remote on his car as he made his way through the parked cars in the lot.

Laurel had vanished. It was just as well. The captivating woman was going to be a challenge, but it would be worth it. If he could find something pointing to Saul in Misty's disappearance, all the better. He would head home, but first, he wanted to stop by the office. There had to be some information out there on his new research partners and he was going to find out what it was.

CHAPTER SIX

LAUREL PULLED HER rolling suitcase out of the trunk of her car and slammed the lid shut. She yanked open the handle and stretched it out, securing her travel tote along the top. Unlike most psychic investigators, she didn't need tons of equipment to take a reading. It was just her and the ghosts. And this morning, a little too much caffeine to cover up the sleepless night she'd had.

She'd given in to her obsessive thoughts about texting Zoe. Still feeling horrible about her accident, she knew Randall and Lowell were taking care of her. But going into a situation without her partner felt strange and she at least wanted her to know where she was in case something went wrong.

I know I promised not to text you for a couple of weeks but I'm about to go into a situation at Greystone and just wanted you to know in case something goes wrong.

She pressed send and put her phone away.

It would be fine. It wasn't like she hadn't done things on her own before. It just felt better when there were two people on the same page. Going anywhere with Gabe when she wasn't sure of his motives was more than a little stressful, especially considering a girl went missing from doing just that.

Letting out a deep sigh, she took another deep breath and got ready to rumble.

Dressed in her favorite gray sweats, a white tank, and her lucky sneakers, she was ready to go. Her hair was pulled back in a simple ponytail. It was easy and she didn't know how long she would have to stay. Simple was always best and damned if she hadn't learned that the hard way.

At least she looked fresh. Thank God for concealer and a cold shower. Meeting Gabe Parsons yesterday had done some strange things to her libido, and even worse, the smug bastard had followed her into her dreams.

"Rough night?" Thickety appeared from the shadows beneath a tree near the fence line and sat grooming his paw.

"Yes. I can't stop thinking about that girl. Misty."

And Zoe.

Thickety's gaze met hers. "I'll be with you. You may not see me, but I won't leave you. Your grandmother was right. This place is riddled with ghosts. The skeptic may scoff, but you need to protect yourself."

"I know."

God, she wished Zoe was here.

She pulled out her tube of lipgloss and applied it as her eyes devoured the scene before her. Greystone Asylum. It was the stuff of her grandmother's nightmares, and if she was to believe Danvers, the possible site of Misty Duncan's death. She thought back to the meeting the day before. Danvers had mentioned Misty Duncan and Parsons had practically taken Saul's face off.

Laurel fingered the beads in her pocket and considered the young assistant. Saul was the kind of guy no one looked at. Brown hair and polite to a fault... at least until someone attacked his professional ethics like she and Parsons had yesterday. Then his mask had slipped just a little. A smile spread across her lips. And here they would have to spend the weekend together. Even better.

"Watch yourself around that one."

"Who?"

Thickety gave her a scornful glance. "Who do you think? Parsons is safe. The other one reeks of desperation."

"For what?"

"I don't know. But I have a feeling you will find that out soon enough. Just keep your wits about you."

Her lips pressed into a thin line, Laurel's thoughts went back to the map of the grounds and the intricate tunnel system beneath the earth. The horrors she had read about the place were legendary. Electroshock treatment, lobotomies, water torture, medical tests without the benefit of sedation, and a whole host of supposed treatments. It was gruesome and horrific.

And her grandmother had been there.

Visions of Nana writhing in the bed as the attendants at the nursing home tried to sedate her brought tears to her eyes.

"Ominous, isn't it?"

The voice startled Laurel and she flinched. Gabe Parsons had parked down the street and somehow gotten his luggage to the gate without her even hearing. Pulse pounding, she flinched and spun around.

"Sneaking up on people is a bad habit to get into." She clenched her teeth to keep from giving him a piece of her mind. If only he didn't make her want to kiss him at the same time as she wanted to punch him in the face.

What was wrong with her?

The man was annoying as hell.

GHOST MOON

He was dressed down today: jeans and sneakers with a tight-fitting T-shirt. But then, he always looked effortless and comfortable on his show.

Sexy bastard.

The sun broke through the early morning clouds, making Laurel glad she wore layers as the heat from the sun and her reaction to Mr. Sexy Britches were making her much too hot for comfort.

Laurel unzipped her hoodie and laid it on top of the rolling suitcase. The air settling over her bare arms was a nice change. She needed the sun on her while she had the chance. There would be no windows where she was going, and if it was anything like her previous cases, the chill would rattle her bones the second she stepped inside the gates.

Death was like that. It called to the ones who heard it best. This place had her rattled.

Thickety gave a warning growl and rubbed against her legs. She reached down as if to scratch her leg and instead ran her hand along his body, a move she'd perfected years ago. It kept her grounded when there were people about.

Parsons wasn't helping her nerves either. She didn't make it a habit to have living color smutterific dreams about guys she didn't like, but this guy had crawled under her skin with the proverbial crowbar. It was, in a word, disturbing.

She didn't know whether to lay him out or investigate the softness factor of his lips... or maybe just how hard his muscles were under that very nice shirt he was wearing.

Choices... choices.

"Sorry. I didn't mean to frighten you." Amusement flickered in the eyes that met hers.

Laurel sighed and shifted her weight, guilt settling through her.

Way to go!

Act like a jerk on the first day, why don't you?

He doesn't need to know the real reason you're cranky.

"I'm sorry. That was totally uncalled for. The least we can do is try and get along during our time on the case. Something happened with my grandmother recently and it has me a little spooked."

"Does she live with you?" Gabe inquired. A polite smile flitted across his features.

"No." Laurel shook her head. "Sometimes, I wish she did, though. I took this job to help get her moved to a different nursing facility." She found it impossible not to answer his smile with one of her own. He was cute when the sun hit his face. The brilliant blue of his eyes snapped in the open air.

"It's quite a large property."

She nodded, chagrined. "Yes. I wonder just how much he expects us to cover. This will be my first case since the accident, and I packed for the weekend."

"You think you can handle it? I mean, after the last one?" His silky voice held a challenge. He nodded his head toward the approaching car. "They're almost here. Last chance."

Laurel narrowed her eyes. What little hold she held on her frayed temper snapped. Self-doubt flared but she stamped it out as quickly as it came. There he was again.

Pompous and condescending.

This Parsons she could deal with. It was a sight better to be angry than scared. Or even looking at him as anything other than someone sent here to shoot her down.

She had half a mind to walk up to the first ghost she came across and grab him by the arm and offer an introduction. With any luck, it would be one with a visage creepy enough to scare him into eating his words.

Asshat.

"What's that supposed to mean?" She stepped forward, hands clenched into fists, her foot brushing against the luggage. Her hoodie slid off the suitcase with an unceremonious flop into the dirt. "We haven't even started on the project and you're trying to displace me already?"

Parsons stepped back, surprise clear on his lightly parted lips. Lips she still wanted to kiss, damn his eyes.

God, what was wrong with her?

Too much work and no play makes Laurel a dull girl.

Damned hormones.

"My friend almost died because of a mistake I made. But you're already aware of that, aren't you, Mr. High and

Mighty? Listen and listen good. I'm here because my grandmother needs me. I'm a damn fine ghost hunter, which you would already know if you bothered to see beyond what happened to Zoe."

She poked her finger into his chest and had the satisfaction of seeing him wince. "In fact, when we get in there and things heat up, you're going to be eating those words. Crow is mighty tasty with a side of ranch, Mr. Parsons. I'll be waiting for that apology, too."

Gabe stepped back and held up his hands, a ruddy flush creeping up his cheeks. "Okay. I was out of line. Truce?"

He bent down and picked up her hoodie, handing it to her.

"Thank you." Laurel snatched the hoodie from his hands and tied it around her waist with a firm yank. She didn't want to chance it falling in the dirt again and it would be a long weekend. At the rate they were going, it would be a full-on ice storm between them.

A flash of humor crossed his face. "Do you think maybe you could call me Gabe?"

"That depends."

"On what?" Gabe cocked his eyebrow.

"On whether you can stop dissecting me like one of your frauds."

"Fraud?" Gabe stepped back. "What are you talking about?"

"You've done nothing but provoke me from the second you got here."

CHAPTER SEVEN

SHE STOOD IN front of him in her tight sweatpants and sneakers with that ridiculous tank top hugging her breasts like it was painted on. He'd spent long hours into the night going over his notes on her last case and still couldn't decide if she was real or just another sad excuse for a human being preying on people at their most vulnerable time.

He had a personal stake in this one.

God help her if he found out she was just here to bilk Danvers. Gabe ran his fingers through his hair and tried to rein in his out of control emotions.

Especially now, when most of his thoughts about her comprised of getting her out of that tank top and seeing just how well those perky breasts fit in the palms of his hands. Let her believe what she wanted. She assumed he was out to get her and that suited him just fine. It would be easier, in fact. Any attraction he felt toward her was skin deep. It had been years since he'd gone out on any kind of date. That's all. She was a pretty face but that was it.

Her eyes flashed violet when she was angry.

Did she realize just how alluring she

looked?

Her gloss-covered lips twisted into a smile that could freeze a man out. Gabe couldn't blame her. He'd been an ass for even asking.

Why would he care?

The press coverage from last year stayed fresh in his mind. Laurel had been involved in a missing persons' case and had traced the abductor to an abandoned building. The child was found, but in the process a wall of the building had collapsed, revealing a cemetery of skeletal remains and nearly killing her best friend Zoe in the process. It was a monumental find. Part of him wondered if she had a hand in the wall coming down. If she had, then she deserved every bit of karma she had coming.

He'd never forget the expression on Laurel's face when the camera crew captured the final footage of the rescue. She'd looked like a refugee from a camp, her hair a stringy mess, face mottled red from crying. And her friend—well, that didn't bear repeating. He doubted her recovery would be a smooth one with the concussion and broken bones. Cement brick was not forgiving.

Laurel moved and the tank tightened against her chilled skin. The thin fabric was no match for the rock hard nipples standing at attention. Gabe's mouth went dry. His dick twitched and he mentally swore. Jesus, the girl could tempt a saint.

Ever since the meeting yesterday he'd

been filled with images of her on the boardroom table, the conservative blue skirt hiked up just past the tops of her stockings. He would run his fingers up the insides of her creamy thighs—

God.

Fucking get a hold of yourself, asshole.

She's a colleague.

Not a conquest.

"Danvers and Saul are here. I suggest you cover up. You've given enough of a show for one day." His expression held a hint of mockery, but he needed to keep her at a distance. If he didn't tamp down on his arousal, it would be one motherfucker of a weekend. If she still thought he was an asshole, so much the better. She would stay out of his way and they'd be able to get their jobs done. "We need to be on our game."

A warning cloud of cold fury settled over Laurel's features. "Fine, *Gabe*. Let's do that." She turned her back on him, viciously slipped the hoodie back on. She gripped her suitcase and stormed down the long driveway toward the gates.

Danvers exited the car. "What was that all about?"

Saul got out and went to the trunk to get his bags for the weekend.

"You don't want to know," Gabe sighed. He picked up his own luggage and followed behind the angry ghost hunter.

God, but she had a sexy ass.

CHAPTER EIGHT

LAUREL STEAMED. SHE knew his gaze was probably focused on her as she made her way down the drive but she didn't care. She had better things to do than spar with the über sexy Gabe Parsons. She could have sworn he was checking her out back there. He'd been looking at her chest.

How dare he?

She stopped in her tracks so

suddenly the suitcase bumped into her foot, knocking her forward a step. Her insides did a wiggly dance and her head spun.

No.

"Was he?" she mused, wrinkling her nose. "No way."

He despised her and assumed she was a fraud, didn't he?

Why else would he be here?

If she was smart, she'd tell Danvers to kiss her backside and find another case. Now, she wanted to prove herself. To let this jerk know just who he was messing with. Sadness weighed her down as thoughts of Zoe settled in. The last time she set out to prove herself it hadn't gone so well.

"He was."

"*Thickety...*"

"Well. He was. Don't get distracted by him, Laurel. You need to stay focused in there."

He was right. She had to keep her shit together. Nana needed her and the smug smile from Parsons was the perfect burr under her proverbial saddle. The way he looked at her... like he could just as easily kiss her as judge her incompetent.

Just you wait, Mr. Parsons.

You have no idea what you're messing with.

But that never stopped a guy from ogling your chest before, right?

Maybe not, but it still irked her just the same.

What right did he have to treat her

like that?

Fury simmered under her skin.

Laurel stared up at the asylum and the hair on the back of her neck shivered. The dead were waiting. Waiting for her. And she would make sure Gabe Parsons got a healthy dose of belief, up close and personal.

The sound of several sets of feet scuffling along in close proximity made her turn around. Danvers, Gabe and Saul had arrived.

"Gentlemen." Laurel nodded. The gate in front of them stood large and foreboding.

"Good morning, Laurel" Danvers reached into his pocket and pulled out the key. "I'm glad to see you're eager to get started. With any luck, this should be a weekend full of answers." He stepped forward and unlocked the wrought iron gate. As he pulled it open, a loud screech rent the air.

Laurel tugged her suitcase behind her and mapped out what she was seeing with the layout from her research. As if reading her mind, Danvers spoke.

"The first building is Greystone House. This was the main nerve center of the asylum, which reaches out for three miles in all directions. There are, as you noted during our conversation yesterday, a series of tunnels beneath the earth where staff members and inmates would move from building to building, completely safe and supervised."

Laurel coughed and cleared her

throat. The structure ahead of her was a dilapidated red brick monstrosity. She counted at least six floors from the outside. The windows were covered with wire-infused safety glass and ivy had grown over part of the building, adding to an air of abandonment.

Danvers led the way onto the property with Saul trailing close behind. Laden with one duffle bag, it was clear he didn't expect to be spending much time at the estate. Their excursion was to be only a couple of days at the most.

"After you." Gabe leaned forward with a gallant swoop of his arm.

"Thank you." Laurel brushed past him, her ears open for anything Danvers could tell them about this place she didn't already know. If the walls echoed as deeply as she assumed they would, Laurel would have her hands full.

She dug into the pocket of her sweatpants and pulled out the wooden bracelet. It looked simple enough, but the ability to center herself was where its power lay. She'd never been on a case without it, and she wasn't about to start now. Thickety trudged along beside her, his presence also calming.

If Parsons was surprised by her distracted response, he said nothing.

"We'll confine your first experience to Greystone House. Saul has the means to get in touch with me, should the need arise." Danvers paused in front of the old building and reached out to clasp Laurel's hand, then Gabe's.

"I trust you'll take care and report

any issue you run up against."

Laurel nodded. She couldn't blame him for wanting to get on with it. "What time will we leave on Sunday, or will it be longer?"

"I'll have the car brought around by ten a.m. Yes. Sunday. Be ready out front near the gate. Rodney, my driver, will have the key." Danvers gave a stern glance in Saul's direction. "Don't be late."

Gabe peered up at the decaying structure. "This is the building where Ms. Duncan began her investigation, if I remember correctly."

Danvers nodded. "It was."

Saul nodded, approaching with the bag. "Yes. It was the last place I saw her before she disappeared."

Laurel moved forward, her gaze drawn to movement from one window upstairs.

"You said there's no caretaker or homeless people inside?" Laurel zipped up her hoodie, suddenly cold.

"Yes. Why?" Danvers replied.

"Because I just caught movement in the fourth floor window." Laurel headed up the stairs, her suitcase bumping along behind her. Let the men talk about maps and structures of the property for hours. She wanted answers and she wasn't going to wait around for another accident. She had her first sighting and she wasn't about to let this one get away.

CHAPTER NINE

GABE WATCHED LAUREL bound up the stairs. After dumping her bag in the front room, she vanished into the shadows. He was convinced now more than ever that Laurel was out of her mind.

"Laurel!"

Not waiting for Saul, he took off after her, depositing his luggage on the floor next to hers. He had to catch up with her. There would be no chance for her to set up any smoke and mirrors. Not on his watch.

"Laurel! Wait!" Damned woman was going to get herself killed. If there was a homeless person lurking in these deserted halls, he didn't want her injured. Gabe picked up speed and took the stairs to the second floor two at a time. If there was an elevator, it had long ago stopped working.

The second and third floors were a blur. As he rounded the fourth floor, he heard a muffled cry. His breathing ragged, he picked up the pace, muscles straining with the need to go faster. His eyes darted down the hallway, debris and abandoned gurneys blocking his passage.

"Laurel?" he called out. "Where are you?"

"Here! I'm in here," came the shaken response.

Gabe propelled himself forward, searching the maze of rooms. Finally, he found her, staring down at Danvers as his driver helped him back into the car and he pulled away. Saul, uncharacteristically sharp in his mannerisms, kicked at the dirt and stalked back up to the house.

"Interesting."

"Quite," he responded. She looked fine, if a little shaken. "Now, could you please tell me what had you so fired up you went up here on your own? What if it had been a homeless person? You could have been hurt."

"I'm sorry." Laurel turned away, rubbing her arms. She looked contrite and her eyes slid away from him.

Gabe frowned. "Did you see something?"

"I'm not sure." She turned her face toward the light and he saw the tired lines around her eyes.

"What did you think it was?" Gabe moved away from the window and surveyed the room, his lip curling at the disarray. "God. This is awful." The smell alone made him want to throw up. Something had died in here, and recently. He hoped it was only an animal. Fresh skeletons were not on his list of hopeful finds.

"It is." Laurel ran her fingers along the leather straps hooked to one of the six beds lined up along the wall. Mattresses torn and stained with long dried fluids lay there, abandoned with their history silent and intact. Broken tile littered the floor, mixed in with soiled bedding and clothing. It was musty and smelled of mildew and darker things.

"I thought I saw someone. A girl."

"Was it Misty?"

Laurel pursed her lips and shook her head. "I don't think so. I've never seen her, though, so I wouldn't know."

"Of course." Gabe felt like a dolt. "She was your height. Short hair. They said she came out here wearing some kind of striped sweater and jeans."

"No." Laurel narrowed her eyes and shook her head. "This girl looked... wilder. More like someone incarcerated here or a resident than someone of our generation, if that makes sense." Her face was pensive and she pulled at the zipper on her hoodie. "She was wearing a brown looking tunic."

Had she really seen something or was she pulling his leg?

Time would tell.

"That sounds like an inmate."

"It does."

"How do you want to do this?" She gave Gabe a tentative smile. "I realize we've kind of gotten off on the wrong foot, but I'm not used to working with someone who hasn't been on my team in some way before."

"I'm not sure I follow." Gabe was intrigued at her change of tactics, if not slightly amused. Just a few minutes before, she'd been haranguing him for daring to insinuate she wasn't up to the task.

Laurel nodded. "Every case I've ever had, had Zoe smack dab in the middle of it. Our research was done beforehand. Together. We mapped out the buildings, plotted sightings. The works. Then it was my turn to go in and see who would come out to play."

"Come out to play?" Gabe raised his eyebrows.

"I don't use equipment for my cases, Mr. Parsons. Gabe. What you see is what you get. No white noise meters to fake out. No cold spots or cameras that go bump in the night. No demon-possessed teenagers calling the devil out for a night on the town. Just me."

"I'll have to see that to believe it." The beginnings of a smile tipped the corners of his mouth. "It just sounds a little too good to be true."

"Ever the skeptic." Laurel sighed. "Okay. This is your chance. You get to see how I solve my cases, but only if you spot me."

Laurel didn't want to like him.

She didn't.

Mostly.

But the way he stood up to her made her blood sing. It was also those little dimples when he smiled like he did just then, and the way his eyes flashed when he was angry. The thick head of hair that just begged her fingers to run through it while she kissed that quirky little grin right off those sexy lips of his.

Her skin warmed at the possibility of where that might lead and a blush crept up the back of her neck.

God, woman.

Get a damned hose.

Thickety roamed the shadows of the room, his red eyes glowing with purpose. He cocked his head and his ear twitched. The demon cat was onto something.

"Spot you? Okay. So just how does that work?" Gabe walked out to the hallway looking back, his gaze rippling over her with hooded eyes.

What the hell is he thinking, staring at me like that?

"You stand still and that's pretty much it. Once I find something or someone who wants to come calling, that is." Her blue eyes met his, playing it cool so he didn't realize how close she was to reaching over and either popping him in the head or planting a kiss on his obstinate lips. She honestly couldn't decide which.

"I know you're here to be the skeptic and that's fine, but I need an anchor. Someone to keep me here, in the present, so I don't get stuck."

Gabe's brows drew downward in a frown. "I don't understand."

She hesitated and sucked in a shaking breath. "No. No one does. That's what landed my grandmother here so many years ago." Laurel laughed, a bitter sound even to her own ears.

"Seeing what others couldn't. The last one nearly claimed me. *God.* The children. That monster..." Her voice wobbled and she pressed her lips together to keep from saying any more. Her stomach heaved at the images of abuse the children had shown her before she freed them from the wall that had been their tomb. It was heartbreaking.

It was the others who were still there that haunted her. The women. One day, she would go back. She had to prove to herself she was strong enough. That house scared her more than Greystone.

"What I need from you is a reference point... and..." Laurel looked away, feeling foolish. This man had worked with every kind of ghost hunter and psychic in the world, and unfortunately, most of them he'd shown to be complete and utter hoaxes. She wanted him to have faith in her. No... *to understand.* He would, in a moment, if he didn't run screaming from the room.

Like her parents.

Like everyone else in her life except her grandmother.

And Zoe.

Laurel cleared her throat and lifted her chin. "I need you to put aside your distrust of me for one minute and just be a man who wants to find the truth."

"How am I supposed to do that?" Gabe held out his arms. "There's nothing to see."

"You haven't tried looking yet."

Gabe approached her and laid a hand tentatively on her arm. His visage was guarded. "What do you need from me, Laurel?"

It was the first kind expression she'd

seen on his face and it was almost her undoing. She turned toward him, her face a mask of determination. "I need you to be there with me so I don't get trapped in the past. Hold me here in the present so I can do what we came here to do."

"How?"

Thickety growled from the murky corners of the room. Something was here and it wanted to say hi. Laurel gave a shaky breath and bolstered up her inner warrior. She could do this.

She gave him a tentative smile. "Just give me your hand."

Laurel sucked in her breath as Gabe slipped his hand in hers. His fingers were warm and strong and a welcome relief from the chill. Since she entered the grounds, hers had gotten colder and she couldn't warm up despite the hoodie. The dead recognized her, and any warmth she had had leached out long ago.

"Jeez. Your hands are like ice."

"Job hazard, I'm afraid." She shrugged, leading him down the hall. Her stomach was still doing somersaults that he was actually holding her hand. Fear churned in her stomach.

What if she couldn't do it?

What if she could?

"Get ready, Laurel," Thickety warned, his tail flicking.

"I think I'd try and renegotiate that one."

Laurel chuckled, relieved at his levity. "I'll take it up with management when we get out of here."

"A solid plan." Gabe followed along closely behind her. "Where do you want to start?"

"Yes, Laurel. By all means. Where would you like to begin? I moved your things into one room upstairs since you bolted up here so quickly." Saul's mouth took on an unpleasant twist.

The demon cat growled low in his throat, putting Laurel on alert. Thickety didn't like Saul one bit. She learned a long time ago to trust her spirit guide and right now, with the way he was pacing and spitting his displeasure, she would bet anything the reason for his reaction was the man who just walked in the room, not the ghosts she sensed drawing near.

They pulled at her, chill fingers brushing against her skin, making her shiver.

Gabe turned toward Saul. "Where have you been?"

"Around." A greasy smile crept across his face.

Laurel's skin crawled. There was something about Saul that set her teeth on edge, but she couldn't put her finger on it. Thickety was right to warn her. Something wasn't right.

Laurel stopped, Gabe still holding her hand. "Where would you suggest, Saul? Since you were the last person to see her alive."

Saul's eyes narrowed, his expression thoughtful. "Danvers wants to be made aware if there are genuine psychic phenomena here. It doesn't matter if we find the Duncan girl."

"It does to me," Gabe snapped. He withdrew his hand from Laurel's and turned to face Saul. "I don't know what game you're playing at, buddy. Misty Duncan was a colleague. She was no fool."

Saul bit back a harsh laugh. "I beg to differ. She went off by herself in this place. That's foolhardy. The girl was a disorganized mess from the get go."

"Not the Misty I knew."

"I can't speak to that, but I can tell you she was way out of her league at Greystone. The ghosts probably ate her alive."

Thickety growled and led Laurel away from the men, disappearing down a dimly lit hallway.

Laurel moved farther down the hall. "Thickety!" she whispered fiercely, but the men were so intent on arguing there seemed little worry in that regard. The cat was after something or someone, and she had to find out what.

As she hurried, her gaze darted around in the gloom. The peeling wallpaper and damaged wooden panels made her sad. Crumbled bits of tile and broken glass littering the floor kept her alert to where she placed her feet. Her sneakers slipped once but she righted herself, a curse at herself for not wearing sturdy work boots on her lips.

Thickety pulled her toward the disturbance, the sensation of drowning in a sea of phantasmagorical energy nearly undoing her. Panic surfaced, and she forced it back down. Losing her shit before she even started was not the way to get the job done.

She needed someone to center her.

Now.

"Where are you?" Gabe's voice echoed down the hall.

"Here."

"Why'd you take off like that?" He was out of breath and the wild look in his eyes revealed his concern.

"I'm sorry. I felt something and had to go." A shadow darted out of the corner of her eyes and the ghostly sound of sobbing reverberated through the open rooms. She took a few steps forward, feeling his warmth behind her.

Laurel stopped in front of a surgical

suite and paused. Thickety stood in front of the door, reaching up with his paw as a sign to go in.

"There's something here I need to see."

"What can I do?"

"Don't let go," Laurel whispered, and slipped her hand in his.

CHAPTER TEN

GABE STEPPED FORWARD and opened the once white painted door. Flakes had fallen off onto the floor, the bare wood discernibly rotten beneath it. "I'll go first. I don't want you to be surprised by someone." He also wanted to make sure everything was clear. No obvious tricks of the trade. The opaque glass window was set with embedded wires to prevent breakage in case of attack but was also designed for no visibility.

Stainless steel equipment gleamed dully beneath their coating of dust. Broken cabinets that once housed equipment, now only held cobwebs and a few random tools scattered by trespassers and curiosity seekers. Asylums were popular with the ghost-hunting crowd. There were so many shows dedicated to sniffing out specters and dredging up things best left undisturbed.

What would they do if they ever came across something real and not a fabric of their imagination?

An examination table sat in the center of the room, the leather straps dangling down like memories of heinous acts long since past.

What kind of surgeries happened here?

From his research, he could guess. The mental health standards during the time Greystone was open were barbaric. Lobotomies, hardcore shock treatment... the works. The pictures he'd looked at online sent chills down his spine. Patients abandoned in rooms to die, still others locked into bathtubs with tarps to secure them in the freezing cold water. Rooms that deprived the criminally insane of all light and sound. It defied reason, the things that went on here.

Gabe scrutinized Laurel as she drew in on herself. She stood stock still, the blood draining from her face leaving her washed out and without color. The air around her vibrated and disembodied voices echoed through the open space.

Surely she hadn't had time to put an audio system in place?

He had been right behind her in the hallway. With the trauma of her accident, he doubted she would come here on her own to tamper with the site.

No.

This was something else.

He yanked his hand out of her grip and stumbled backward. Laurel moaned and her hands clenched into fists. He blinked and searched the room for Saul. If he'd been behind them, he'd most likely stepped out of the room in disgust at watching him hold Laurel's hand like some kind of idiot.

Fine.

Gabe would play her game until he

had enough rope to hang her with.

"Laurel?"

She didn't answer, her gaze locked on something ahead of her that only she could see.

Gabe stepped closer but hesitated to touch her. She appeared fragile enough to break. He gingerly reached out and laid his hand on her forehead. She was frigid. Freezing. He drew his hand back with an intake of breath and gritted his teeth.

This was odd.

He walked around her and scanned the walls and floors.

Nothing.

No wires, no air drafts.

He wasn't prepared for this. Gabe had seen no documentation of her lapsing into any kind of fugue state, and he'd researched the hell out of this woman. The injury from the last case made it imperative to find out all he could about his new "partner" on this case. If he was going into the dark with someone, he would make damned well sure who. Her not appearing to have any involvements in her life, save for a grandmother she cared for, was an unexpected relief. That still didn't make her an honest ghost hunter.

Her spark got under his skin. Most women he encountered bowed and scraped to his celebrity status. Laurel didn't. She was beautiful and smart and right now was scaring the holy fucking hell out of him.

Was that the difference here?

That she didn't have Zoe to act as the buffer from whatever it was she was experiencing?

Was she some kind of psychic, too?

Her lips, now turning blue, moved but there was no sound.

"Laurel?"

Nothing.

His guts twisted inside of him.

Gabe tipped her chin up to search her eyes. He wasn't sure what he was looking for, but as he gazed into the blue depths of her glassy orbs, his perception of reality tilted. Something flickered behind her gaze that drew him down into another time. Another reality. Voices and echoes of the past stormed past his defenses and he stood, not in a derelict building, but a busy operating room.

"Nurse. Get me the ether," a man wearing a white coat and blue face mask demanded, his white eyebrows turned down in irritation.

"Yes, doctor." A dark-haired nurse in a white cap hurried to do his bidding. She scurried to a counter at the back of the room, dodging three other nurses, each intent on whatever job they were performing. The nurse returned quickly with the mask and the bottle.

"You." He pointed at the youngest of the four. A sallow-faced woman with mousy brown hair smoothed her hands along her apron and waited for whatever abuse was about to be heaped on her. "Get out of the way. We have a sterilization procedure at one-thirty." The doctor slid the mask over the woman's face. "Go ready the patient in 4B. I'll be with her shortly."

The female patient strapped to the chair writhed against the restraints, her eyes wide and terrified. Gagged, she tried to speak but a line of spittle slid down her cheek as he affixed the mask over her face. Her eyelids fluttered and her face went slack as the effects of the chemical took over.

"You have been an atrocious wife, Frau Gilbert. Trying to escape when all your husband wanted from you is your obedience. But lucky for you, I have the perfect remedy for willful women such as yourself." The doctor roughly gripped her face and moved it back and forth.

The woman lay still and unresponsive. The doctor removed the mask.

"Tray! Alcohol!" The next gruff orders and the remaining nurses scattered to gain said items.

Gabe blinked, trying to wrap his mind around what was happening. His stomach churned with fear and the hair on his arms stood up.

Where the fuck was he?

No.

The question was more like *when.*

He was there.

With Laurel.

In the past.

It was impossible.

Wasn't it?

Is this how she found the missing boy and all those other people?

Living through horrors to find them?

What had she seen at the Barker house to drive her into not taking cases?

It was more than just her partner getting injured. This... whatever this was. Her way of seeing the dead. It was there. In your face. No holds barred.

"Oh God," he whispered, the terror sinking in.

This was fucking real.

She was real.

He faced Laurel and still held her face in his hands. Gabe moved away, but remembering her warning didn't break contact. He slid his hand down her shoulder and took her clammy hand in his. Maybe if he continued touching her, it would generate a response.

Something.

Anything.

Oh my God.

Gabe's stomach curdled and he struggled with the urge to vomit.

"Laurel," he hissed. "Where are we?"

"They can't hear us," she responded, her voice flat. "I'm sorry. I took us back too far. I was thinking of my grandmother and I must have overshot." She stared hard at the woman in the chair, completely transfixed.

"He'll really do it." Gabe's eyes took in the scene in front of him and he drew his lips back in horror. "He's going to give her a lobotomy right here."

"Yes." A tear slid down Laurel's face and she wiped it away with an angry swipe of her hand. "This is what my grandmother had to live through. This place. That... monster."

"Can we do anything?" Gabe watched, powerless, as the nurses pushed the equipment up next to the chair and the doctor took his place. He felt the helplessness settle over him and took a haggard breath. This was what she went through. He didn't comprehend how she stood it without going mad.

"I'm not sure." Laurel let her gaze flit up to meet his, her eyes blinking with wonder. "I've never brought anyone with me before."

"What about Zoe?"

"She kept me grounded in the present. Let me see the ghosts but never came with me."

"Let me try." Gabe started to let go of her hand. "Maybe we can get her out of here."

"No!" Laurel choked out, her eyes wild. "Don't let go. If you let go, we'll be trapped here."

"How do you know."

"I..." Her voice broke. "It's something my grandmother warned me about. To never let go. If this happened."

So, it ran in her family.

Interesting.

He wanted to meet this grandmother of hers.

"Okay. Okay." He drew her against his chest and smoothed his hand down the back of her head. "I'm sorry. I won't." He felt like a horrendous shit for doubting her, but he had to know.

"Don't. We have to stick together." Laurel pulled back and met his eyes, her hand sliding into his. "If I get stuck, then so do you."

Laurel followed behind Gabe, their hands joined, as he tested out his theory by waving a hand in front of the doctor. He picked up the tray and moved it, only to find it right back where it was a second before.

"We can't effect change. We can observe. At least, that has been my experience before." Laurel sighed, giving voice to the frustration. "I have to get us back to when Misty went missing. It shouldn't take us long. But seriously, let's get out of here. I can't watch."

"I'm with you." Gabe shuddered, his face pinched with anger. "No wonder this place was shut down." He paused. "I owe you an apology. I spent so many cases with hucksters and cheats, I couldn't see what was real right under my own nose."

Laurel let a small smile play across her lips. "You needed to *see*." She looked away as a prickle of tears threatened to break her composure.

How long had she waited to hear that from someone who might be able to understand what it was like for her?

"I could have been here if it weren't for my grandmother."

"What do you mean?"

"My parents. They had me locked up and *evaluated*."

"What are you talking about?"

"It was nothing like this, at least." Laurel swallowed.

"This place has been closed down for a long time."

"No..." Laurel shook her head, trying

to find the right words. "When my parents found out I could see the dead, talk to them... they tried to have me committed. I went to live with Nana. Without her, I would be that woman on the bed, strapped down and getting ready for a needle to be shoved in my eye socket. Stepford daughter, at your service." She let out a nearly hysterical laugh.

Did she dare tell him about Thickety?

Could he even see him?

The cat swished his tail, his red eyes glowing from the small black face.

"I'm sorry." Gabe's voice was thick and he looked away. "I treated you like shit."

"You haven't seen it all yet." Laurel led him into the hall, trying to shake off the joy at his comments.

He believed her.

Patients sat forgotten in wheelchairs, cries from the rooms echoing down the hallway. No longer littered with broken tile, they could wind their way through the sedentary people and head deeper into the building. "I hit Google when I heard from Danvers and after talking with my Nana."

Gabe nodded. "I did some research when Misty disappeared. I couldn't believe he wanted to have a theme park here, of all places. The pain these people suffered. It just made little sense to me at the time." They passed a room with a woman screaming. The lights flickered off and on. "I don't want to even guess what's going on in there."

"Don't. We have to move. I don't want us in a dangerous part of the building when we resurface." Her stomach twisted and she sucked in a shaky breath.

"Okay. Now what?"

"We try and go back to when Misty vanished. If we can retrace her steps or at least get a glimpse of her, then we could maybe figure out what happened." Her thoughts were racing.

What if I can't find her?

This place is huge and there is no guarantee she stayed here and didn't go wandering the tunnels or even to one of the other buildings.

CHAPTER ELEVEN

LAUREL WATCHED GABE'S face. His jaw was clenched tight and his gaze darted around their surroundings, as if trying to piece it all together. Still, with his hand wrapped around hers, she felt more calm than afraid. Like together they might be able to do this. He didn't understand it.

How could he when she didn't understand it herself?

But the fact that he was on her side now, made all the difference in the world.

Thickety made a retching sound and she shot him a look.

"Shut up."

"What?"

"Not you."

"Umm. Okay."

More retching. "I'm going to tell him if you don't shut up."

"Who are you talking to?"

Laurel looked down at her feet then back up to his face. "When I told you my parents locked me up, it wasn't just for seeing dead people. I... and, well, my grandmother, too, if you want to know the truth, have a spirit guide that sort of helps us along when things get a little, um... difficult."

"How?"

"It's just something I've been able to do since I was little. My grandmother helped me. And um... Thickety."

"Who's Thickety?"

The cat's eye burned into her then he sighed. "The demon standing to your left. Black cat. Red eyes."

"Shit!" Gabe stepped back and nearly let go of her hand. His eyes widened and his mouth dropped open, gaping like a fish.

"Thickety! That wasn't nice."

The demon snorted. "Nice isn't in my vocabulary. I was testing him to see if he could hear me. You *can* hear me. But can you *see* me?"

His eyes searched hers, glittering

bright in the half-light of the hallway. Then his gaze shifted to Thickety. "I can. This is getting more disturbing with every second, you do realize that don't you?"

A nervous laugh bubbled out from between Laurel's lips. "You have no idea."

"Nice to meet you, Thickety."

The cat growled and shuffled down the hall in front of them. "Can we get a move on, please? There is some essence of time involved, you know."

"A demon cat? How did that happen?"

"I don't know how exactly." Laurel shrugged. Her lips twisted into a semblance of a smile. "But I'm glad you're here. Both of you."

Gabe froze mid-step, trying to block

her view. "We should turn around."

"Why?" She pushed past him but he maneuvered into her path, giving her hand a tug.

"Let her see, Parsons." Thickety ground out. "It's part of the reason she's here."

"No. Laurel, come on. We need to go the other way." He tried to lead her, but Laurel squirmed around him and her gaze fell on the scene in front of her.

"You two are going to drive me insane." She poked her finger into Gabe's arm. "Stop dragging me around. And you..." Laurel pointed at Thickety. "Stop being so cryptic."

"Laurel..."

"What?" Then, she glanced up.

CHAPTER TWELVE

GABE TRIED TO shield Laurel but she was too fast. He recognized the woman strapped down, screaming curses in German. The door was open and the woman was laid out, ankles and wrists bound by leather straps. It was room 4B. Sterilization set for 1:30, according to the doctor. Icy chills raced up his back.

Oh shit.

I know that face, but more importantly

so does Laurel.

Laurel stood in the doorway, slack-jawed, an expression of horror on her face. Tears pooled in her bright blue eyes and she let them fall unchecked.

"Nana?" Laurel breathed. She turned her head sharply to glance at him.

"She looks so young."

He couldn't meet her eyes. His research had been thorough. Gabe had searched through records on the asylum's history the night before and he'd come across her grandmother's name. It had triggered something in his memory. Not realizing what alerted him, he poured over his notes from Greystone and there she was.

Gretchen Krause.

Laurel's Nana.

"Who are you?" the woman on the bed spat out. "You want to stare at the crazy girl, go ahead. I have no dignity left." Her blonde hair was long and stringy and the hospital gown did little to protect her modesty.

"Oh my God. You can hear us?"

"I can hear you, silly girl. I'm crazy but I'm not deaf." The woman's eyebrows turned down in irritation.

Laurel's mouth dropped open.

"Leave your mouth open like that, you'll catch a fly," Gretchen snorted.

"Gabe, how did you know?"

"I saw the list last night when I was doing more research. The name was familiar so I looked it up. It was your grandmother." He sighed and ran his fingers roughly through his hair. "I

183

didn't want you to have to see her like this."

"Come with me."

"Visiting the crazy girl? How nice you are," Gretchen sniped, her eyes darting from Gabe to Laurel.

Thickety roamed into the room and Gretchen's eyes froze on him. "Where is Jasper?"

"He's here. Somewhere. It's the only reason I'm still sane." Gretchen's words were soft but Gabe heard her. "You... I know you."

"You can't touch anything and make it stick. But maybe with you here, I can."

Gabe rubbed his face. "Why would that work?"

"Because you shouldn't have been able to come with me. No one ever has before. Not Zoe. Not Nana. Not ever. Until you." Laurel met his gaze. "I need your help. Are you at least willing to try?"

Gabe gazed into Laurel's eyes and felt something inside of him shift. It wasn't just the way the light fell against the bloom in her cheeks or the way she refused to acquiesce to him.

No.

The more he was finding out about this incredible woman, the more he wanted to bury his fingers in her hair and kiss the daylights out of her.

"I am." Gabe turned to Gretchen. "Ms. Krause, we need you to lie still for a moment." He tugged Laurel into the room and pointed at the door. "Here's your first test. Try and shut it."

CHAPTER THIRTEEN

LAUREL NIBBLED ON her lip. She'd never been able to effect change in the past. Gabe being able to follow her, gave a girl reason to hope. Sometimes, all it took was one wild card. He not only believed her now, he was trying to help. Heat traveled through her body at the thought.

Focus, Laurel.

She glanced at her watch and her

blood ran cold. It was almost time for them to come for the sterilization. "Oh no!" She hastily shoved against the door, to no avail.

"Hurry, Laurel." Gabe's voice was urgent. He placed his own hands on top of hers, but that had no success either. He growled under his breath and snatched his hands away in irritation.

Shit.

Her thoughts raced. If she let him go things could go horribly wrong. Except Thickety and Nana were here. That might just even the scales. And Jasper was someplace close.

What if she took something of his and used it as an anchor instead?

The idea had merit.

How far could they get holding hands

like two idiots?

"Do you have a quarter?"

"You going to make a phone call?"

"Ha ha. No."

Gabe slid his hand in his pocket and slipped the warm coin into her open hand. It worked in *Somewhere in Time,* so maybe it would work the same way here. All she would have to do is look at the coin and think of him and it would take her back.

Them.

It would take *them* back.

"Let go of my hand."

Gabe stared at her like she'd slapped him. "You said not to." Gabe hesitated and his fingers wrapped tighter around hers in protest.

"I know what I said." Laurel reared up

again to push but nothing happened. "What if we're keeping each other from doing something because we're touching? Locked in our reality, but in this time, nothing could happen? I think having a piece of physical essence from home might just work."

"You'll strand us here." Gabe's voice was quiet and his expression stilled and grew serious. "You said it yourself. Don't let go or we'll be trapped."

"I don't think that will happen. Not with something to tie us together and to the present."

"Listen to the girl." Gretchen Krause spoke up from the bed, her eyes wide with shock. "You—you share my gifts? Who are you?" Her fingers bit into the mattress.

Laurel and Gabe walked closer to the bed. She gripped his strong hand in hers and was grateful he hadn't let go when she told him to. It was frightening how attached she was getting to the handsome researcher. He accepted her freakishness and hadn't run screaming. She was trying to be positive.

Tears of love prickled against Laurel's eyes. "I'm your granddaughter, Laurel. We've been sent here to solve a murder, but I had to see you." She drew a strangled breath and willed her emotions under control. "You told me about this place and I couldn't get what you said out of my mind. I let it steer me here instead of the time we should have gone to. We're here to investigate a death and prove just how haunted the asylum really is." She slipped her fingers into her grandmother's hand. "I can't leave you here." Her voice hiccupped. "I just can't."

"Then don't, *liebchen*," the younger version of Nana answered. "You remind me so much of my grandmother. Your eyes. And this place... it reeks of the dead. So many." She blinked back tears and looked away. "My mother sent me here. I wouldn't marry the man they chose. So, I must be made to heel. Like a dog."

"So that's why. I wondered." Laurel sucked in a breath. "But we have to get you out of here. I just don't know how. The fact that you can see me—"

"Let his hand go. You will be able to go back once you join hands again. You carry my blood. This can be done with someone you have a strong connection with." Gretchen's eyes traveled over Gabe then flickered back to Laurel. "Strong. Yes." A twinkle of mischief sparkled in the young woman's eye.

"I have to try, Gabe. Stay with me?" Laurel pleaded. "I can't do it alone, but I have to try this."

"I hate to break it to you, but if we don't move now, this won't end well." Thickety edged toward the door. Jasper appeared, his marmalade form a wisp of smoke and ash in the fetid air of the room.

"What can I do?"

"Help us get her out." Thickety's tail swished and he poked his head into the hall.

His fingers slipped from hers, a pained expression on his face. The absence of warmth sent a shiver down her spine but as she met her grandmother's eyes, Laurel understood why she'd come back.

Her shaking hands pushed the door and it moved.

"Oh, my God."

"Can you watch out the window, Gabe? Let me know if someone's there?"

Gabe nodded and stepped to the door, pressing his face to the glass.

Laurel smiled as she knelt over her grandmother. "I couldn't leave you." Her fingers gripped the thick leather straps and pulled them loose. The first wrist strap came free and Laurel moved to the foot of the bed, freeing the first ankle from its binding. She hurried to the next two and soon, Nana sat up. She swung her legs over the edge of the bed, her feet tentatively touching the floor.

"Someone's coming," Gabe whispered.

Laurel tensed, pulling her grandmother up onto her feet. "We have to hurry. If they take you..." The horror of what could happen slithered through Laurel's brain. They were about to sterilize her grandmother. But only if they caught them.

"Oh my God. Gabe—" Her gaze searched out his, panic rising in her gut.

"I know," was his grim response. "If we don't get her out of here, there's a danger they'll find her and go through with their procedure."

"They can't." Laurel pressed her lips

together in grim determination.

"What procedure?" Gretchen asked. She shuffled across the floor, each step gaining traction. Her footing still slightly unsteady, she leaned on Laurel's arm. Uneven sunlight flickered through the safety glass, showing the afternoon light was fading. Thunder boomed in the distance and rain pelted the glass.

"How long have we been here?"

Laurel shook her head. "I don't know. Time should be the same, but I never had cause to consider it before. We have to go. Now." Wrapping her arm around her grandmother's waist, she urged her toward the door.

"There is a tunnel that leads out from the laundry and the kitchen. I've seen them. They bring in the supplies and take out the bread and linens. I watch them go in and out, but with the drugs they give us, they think we don't notice. One time, I followed and they caught me. Dr. Gering was most displeased." Gretchen shuddered, her face contorting into a mask of bitterness.

"Is it clear?"

Gabe twisted his head. "Yes." He motioned with his hands. "You're going to have to open the door. I can't."

Laurel nodded. "Let's go. The tunnel is the only way."

CHAPTER FOURTEEN

GABE GUIDED THE two women down the hallway, stepping around the people tossed away like refuse. They had been lucky so far, but in a building this full of staff and inmates, their luck wouldn't hold forever.

"Take the elevator. I will lie to the orderly. Say I am due in the laundry for work," Gretchen volunteered, her pace picking up. "They know me."

"Good. Let's go."

"Hold his hand, *liebchen*. They can't see you here or it will not go well for you or me. Sneaking strangers onto the property is *verboten*."

"Okay." Laurel slid her hand into Gabe's and he marveled at how strong these two women were in the face of such danger. He followed behind Gretchen and held Laurel back as she approached the orderly guarding the elevator.

"Good afternoon. I am requested in the laundry, it seems. May I go down, please?" Gretchen kept her head down and her hands clasped together in front of her.

A plump guard waved her on. "Yes. Go. I heard one machine is down. You girls will have a long night."

Gretchen hurried into the elevator car. Laurel and Gabe scurried in as the doors shut. Gabe cradled Laurel's body against his in the tight space. She was so warm and the strawberry scent of her shampoo went right to his groin.

Clearing her throat, Gretchen shot an elbow out and connected with Gabe's ribs.

"Oww," he grunted and backed away, putting air between him and Laurel.

The woman in question chuckled dryly. "Nana," she scolded. "That wasn't nice."

"You two need to get a room." Jasper snickered, moving close beside Gretchen.

Gretchen sniffed and strode to the

front of the car. The elevator shuddered to a halt and she got out, the two time travelers following behind her unseen.

The cavernous room was abuzz with people and the smell of water and wet clothing. Large vats of water were in use. Inmates washed and rinsed the linens as another inmate passed them down to be placed in the industrial-sized dryers. At another station, women lined up against long metal tables and folded laundry, passing it down to be placed in a large cart.

Gretchen led them to a full laundry cart and pushed. The mouth of the tunnel was just beyond the last group of women. The guard who should have been there was next to the washing machine yelling at a repairman. Silent washing machines lined one end of the room, broken and useless.

"Do you have any idea how many inmates we have here? I can't have these women down here stirring this shit in vats all day and night. We need these machines working."

"Tell that to the management upstairs. They've only authorized a certain amount of money and that ain't gonna fix nothing. Let the crazies stir. It gives them somethin' to do."

"I ought to report you." The guard spit on the floor. "No good asshole. Just get out."

"I'm leaving, but that won't change anything." The repairman walked out, shaking his head, the guard following closely behind. "No good bastards. Want something for nothing."

The laundry cart squeaked and rattled as it went into the mouth of the tunnel, Gretchen pushed it as fast as she could go without arousing suspicion. Laurel and Gabe kept up with her brisk pace, the two cats trotting behind them.

Laurel started as something furry ran in front of the large white laundry cart. The lighting was dim and gave an ominous flicker. The floor was slick and she didn't even want to consider what was covering the uneven bricks.

"It is here I can leave you. The door, it opens there." Gretchen stopped, her face an unreadable mask.

"I'm glad we were here to help you." Laurel approached her grandmother and wrapped her arms around her in a hug.

It was still strange to see her so young.

"I too, *liebchen*." Gretchen pulled away. "Now, hurry. I must go or they will find me. The storm will shield my movement from the guards outside."

"I love you," Laurel murmured, pressing a kiss to her cheek. "Go. I'll see you soon."

"Of that, I have faith." Gretchen leaned back and brought a hand up to caress Laurel's face. "How beautiful you are. Now, go." She held her hand out to Gabe. "Take her and do what you came to do. Then, go back to your time and take care of her. You will make a good couple, I think."

"If you don't hurry, you won't have to worry for long," Thickety snarked, his ears perking up at something at the end of the tunnel.

Gabe nodded, his face grim. "Be careful."

"You also." Gretchen released them both and without a word, slipped into the shadows and out a door Laurel hadn't even noticed was there. Jasper followed close behind, vanishing into the murky dark.

"Wow." Her voice shook. She wrapped her arms around her waist and leaned into Gabe.

A couple?

It was all so much to take in.

"She's gone." Laurel let the tears flow, happiness and sadness mixing into an incomprehensible quagmire of emotion.

"Come here." He wrapped his arms around her.

The heat from his embrace melted the cold that filled her soul. This place was horrible and she couldn't wait to leave. The important thing was, she had helped her grandmother survive and ensured she would be there when they got back to the future.

"We have to get back to our time. I don't know how long we've been gone. Saul will wonder if we've vanished, too."

"I'm not worried about Saul. I'm worried about you." Gabe tilted her chin up and captured her lips with his.

His lips were just as warm and sinful as she'd been hoping. Liquid heat spread through her body and she pressed herself in closer. His hardness was a perfect foil for her curves and she groaned into his mouth.

Emotions took over as her fingers reached up and moved through his hair. She shivered against him and pressed harder into his obvious arousal. Insta love wasn't something she was entirely comfortable with, but she figured they would have time to explore their options when they got back. That was something she was distinctly looking forward to.

"I'm glad we don't hate each other anymore," she purred, snuggling into his arms and lifting her face for another panty-soaking kiss.

"Me too." Gabe broke away, blinking in the dim light. "You don't know how much I want to do this, but not here and definitely not right now. We have to find Misty and get back with some answers for Danvers."

Laurel panted, her body aflame with desire. She wanted to kiss him again and dare him to say no. Her breasts tightened against his chest. He was right. The closeness and stress was making their connection stronger in her mind, but still. He smelled so very... well... lickable.

"I—"

"Laurel—God. Let's get walking before I do something I'll regret." Gabe tugged her hand and they continued down the dark tunnel, the musty scent of rot and decay getting stronger the deeper they went. "I don't want our first real kiss to be in a grungy tunnel."

"Get a room. If you don't, I may have to gouge out my eyes."

"Oh, shut up, Thickety."

She was so focused she almost didn't notice the shift in temperature and the different vibration of the air around them. "Do you feel it?"

"What?" Gabe stopped and looked back but she could hardly see his face.

"We're in a different time."

CHAPTER FIFTEEN

GABE ALMOST SWALLOWED his tongue. "We're what?"

"We shifted time. Didn't you notice the lights?" Laurel chortled under her breath. "Thank goodness."

"No. I was too busy thinking about not kissing you." *And shoving you up against some filthy tunnel wall and burying myself in your heat.*

"Oh." She giggled, trudging up behind

him.

"You're giggling? Now?"

Laurel snorted. "I'm sorry. I didn't think you wanted to kiss me all that much. You kind of walked away pretty fast back there."

Gabe stared at her, incredulous. "I've got news for you. Since you came flouncing into the conference room in that painted-on suit, I've thought of little else but bending you over that damned conference table and finding out just what your lips tasted like. Among other things." His body hardened at the thought and he had to keep walking.

"Even though you thought I was a fake?" She paused and batted her eyelashes. "Oh." Laurel stopped, her eyes meeting his. "Then I guess I should mention I wanted you to. Kiss me that is..." She paused, giving him a flirty glance. "What other things?"

Gabe groaned. "This is not supposed to be happening." He strode up to Laurel and mashed his lips against hers in a kiss that was nothing short of possession. Urging her mouth open with his tongue, he stroked hers, winding their essences together, eliciting a groan from deep down in her core.

His hands cupped the soft globes of her breasts and his erection pressed against the softness of her taut belly. She met his passion, kiss for kiss, melding her body against his.

She broke free of the kiss with a gasp. "I want you."

Gabe closed his eyes and let himself

surrender to the spell of her scent. His jeans were getting uncomfortably tight, and all he could think about was how soon they could end this and find someplace to be alone so they could get to know each other better.

Much, much better.

"Wow." The sound of clapping filled Gabe's ears and he tore his lips away from Laurel to find they had an audience. She looked familiar. His fingers tightened on Laurel's upper arms and he blinked to be sure he was seeing what and who he thought he was.

"Misty?"

"In the flesh. Or... not so much." Misty rolled her eyes and gave a deep sigh. "How are you, Parsons? A quest for romance in the tunnels of Greystone. I have to say, that's an original plan. The man who never dates finding love among the rats."

Misty chuckled and came closer. Short brown hair cut into a bob bounced as she drifted toward the couple. Muddy jeans, sneakers and a soiled sweater covered her pale blue-tinged skin.

Young and irreverent, just like he remembered her. "Misty."

"You're Misty Duncan?" Laurel stepped out of Gabe's embrace and held out a hand to Misty in greeting.

"I am. And you are why I'm here, I expect." Misty smiled, a sad expression sliding over her face.

Laurel nodded. "We were sent here by Danvers to finish what you started."

Gabe cleared his throat and joined

them. "You look good, kid. I'm sorry about what happened." It saddened him to see her this way.

"Me too." Misty gazed down the tunnel. "This is not where I planned to spend eternity, I'll give you that." Her visage flickered and diminished.

"Laurel?" Gabe panicked. "She's fading."

Laurel ran her hand along Gabe's arm. Misty sharpened back into focus.

"Can you tell us what happened?" Gabe moved closer. It was surreal talking to a ghost, especially one he knew. It had to be Laurel. She brushed up against him and placed her hand in his and the image of Misty grew stronger.

"Well that should be obvious, even to

you." Thickety's red eyes were luminous in the darkness with only the vague flickering light of the tunnel.

Misty shook her head. "I was irritated with Saul... I remember that much. He was on the phone with someone, arguing, and I walked away. We had a job to do and I wasn't going wait for him to finish his business transaction."

"Business transaction?" Gabe's focus sharpened. "What did you hear?"

Misty ran her hand down the side of her face. "I think he was talking to someone about buying this place out from under Danvers once the sale finally went through. He wanted it for himself. The buildings, the plan to make it into a tourist trap. The whole thing."

Laurel turned to Gabe. "What would a

nothing guy like that want Greystone for? He could just get investors. Why go to the trouble of going behind Danvers' back?"

Gabe narrowed his eyes and stared down the tunnels. His mind was racing. Something about the guy had bothered him from day one but he couldn't lay his finger on what it was.

"How would an assistant get enough money?" Gabe's mind raced.

If the property were a crime scene maybe?

Or if it was proven to be unsafe to the point that Danvers didn't want it?

Only that didn't work, now did it.

"The tunnels." Misty walked back and leaned against the wall. "You forget I've had time to become familiar with my new, um... home."

"Why the tunnels? I don't understand." Laurel shook her head. "It's disgusting down here. The smell. The rats. The history."

"He's using them to hide drugs. Saul James is the biggest meth dealer this side of the state." Misty frowned, her eyes narrowing in thought. "I took a while to figure it out. Why he was here day and night." She blinked and shrugged. "He must have thought I'd seen something when I was wandering the tunnels that last day. The rest is foggy. I remember arguing with him and then... well... nothing."

Gabe nodded. "It makes perfect sense."

"How did you figure out about the

meth?" Laurel wrapped her arm around Gabe.

"That awesome ghostly invisibility cloak thing can be useful. To a point." Misty made a face. "That man was always on the phone. Deals and dealers popping in at all hours. The place should be called Grand Central Station."

"What if he finds us?" Laurel intoned. "He'll think we're on to him, too."

"Too late." Thickety growled, drawing closer to Laurel.

Another noise from the opposite part of the tunnel had Laurel craning to see in the darkness.

A flashlight beam bobbled in the distance, but it was Randall bounding up the tunnel with Lowell in tow that got her to smile. The two ghosts seemed to be getting along. At least for now.

"You found us."

"Of course, we did." Randall scoffed. "But really, did you have to pick the grossest place in the whole hospital?"

"He's not wrong." Lowell tightened his lips, his eyes searching for Zoe. "They're over here."

"Hi." Zoe moved slowly, her right arm in a sling and her left leg in a boot.

"Omg. You didn't have to come down here."

A huge eyeroll was her only response as she huffed and puffed, moving slow and steady in their direction.

"Laurel? Gabe? Are you down here?" Saul's voice drifted down the tunnel. A shadow was making its way toward them, footsteps echoing in the hollow space.

"That's great that you have help, but we better get you out. Now." Misty's eyes narrowed.

"We came here to see what happened to you," Laurel countered.

"Thank you. I'm tied to this place, or, it seems, someone like you with that great psychic connection." Misty gazed at the approaching shadow, a look of contempt in her eyes. "You'd better go." She pushed away from the wall. "Before he sees you."

"The ghost is right. He means you harm." Thickety hissed, pacing back and forth.

Laurel froze, her eyes locking on Gabe's, then moving toward Zoe's.

"Are you deaf? Unless you want to be

a permanent fixture down here with me, I suggest you take the exit your grandmother took." Misty stalked forward toward the shadow, her stride angry and expression hard.

"*He* killed you," Laurel whispered, horror spreading across her face. "Oh my God."

"Killed who?" Saul stepped from the shadows, training a flashlight in Laurel, Zoe, and Gabe's startled eyes.

Laurel and Zoe backed away as Misty stalked an unsuspecting Saul like a caged lion.

"Now who is this? I don't recall her being on the payroll."

"She's one of my team members," Laurel interjected.

"Really. You're holding hands now?

Wow, Parsons, that was fast." Saul laughed, a cold, slimy sound that slithered all the way down Laurel's spine. "And here I thought you would help me prove the little slut was a fake, just like the last one."

"What are you doing here, Saul? We were coming back up. Nothing to see. We really don't need any help down here."

"Ah. But I think you do." Saul stepped forward, a menacing smile turning up the corners of his mouth. "The tunnels... well, they're not good for your health. People have died mucking around in places they don't belong."

"You don't say?" Gabe replied dryly. "I think it's time we go back up to the house and discuss our findings. We still have a lot of ground to cover." He tugged

Laurel after him but stopped as he heard the hammer being pulled back on a gun.

"No. Sadly, that's not part of the plan."

Laurel gasped as Gabe thrust her behind him. "Go," he whispered. "Run. Get help." She staggered backward and fell against the slimy concrete wall. Icy fear bathed her body, and she couldn't get her limbs to move fast enough.

Thickety growled, his rage palpable. His eyes snapped and his size shifted into a larger version of himself. "Don't get too far away from me, Laurel."

"I won't but, God, Thickety. Help him."

Zoe's gaze searched Lowell's and Randall's and they moved closer, waiting for the right moment.

"Let us go."

"I don't think so, Parsons. You've been down in the tunnels. I can't have that." A shot rang out through the enclosed space, the sound deafening.

Gabe froze, his body folding down onto the refuse-covered passage.

"Oh my God." Laurel scooted in reverse on her butt and hands, trying to right herself so she could run. "Gabe!"

"Oh my God," Zoe whispered, backing into the tunnel wall.

Saul kicked Gabe with his shoe. His body moved, but he didn't respond.

"Don't worry, princess. He's not dead yet. Give him time. I'm sure you two will have lots to talk about in the years to come, since you've gotten so chummy."

Tears of anger gathered behind

Laurel's lids but she quickly blinked them away.

He shot Gabe.

Misty too.

Laurel gripped the wooden beads in her pocket and tried to think rationally. It was dark and dank, and he had them trapped. The only advantage she had was her link to the dead.

Misty.

Randall.

Lowell.

Laurel spied Misty next to Gabe, kneeling at his side. Her lips were drawn down in a frown and she shook her head.

Randall and Lowell hovered nearby as if they weren't sure what to do or where to go.

"Oh God."

"Come on. Get up. I'm not dragging both of you. Do you even know how fucking exhausting that is? The Duncan bitch was bad enough. Three tunnels and a nice ready-made bog near the lake. It couldn't be more perfect. Your boyfriend here jumped the gun, but you, you'll walk it and you and your friend can help me carry him."

"What? Zoe can't carry anything."

"You heard me." Saul loomed in front of her as he yanked her arm and dragged her off the slime-covered floor with one vicious pull.

"Come on, Prince Charming. Get up or your fair maiden will get a slug right in the leg just to make it interesting."

Gabe groaned and tried to move.

"Gabe!" Laurel choked out a sob. "Are you okay?"

"No," came the raspy response.

Saul prowled closer to Gabe.

"On second thought, I think I'll just kill you here. Let them think you're a homeless person out for a scare fest. Poor little wino who got lost in the tunnels. No one will care. Especially with your lady love dead." Saul kicked him again. "No one will miss you, Parsons. You're a bastard with a hard-on for pointing out other people's flaws." He chuckled. "You're sad, man."

"No!" Laurel scrambled up from where she was sitting and scanned the floor for something to use against him. Anything. There, propped against the wall, was a shovel. Her eyes darted toward it, calculating if she could reach it before he figured out she'd moved. He was so intent on his revenge on Gabe, it might work.

"Thickety, help me."

"He's mine," Misty growled, floating over. "Get the shovel. I used it to dig around for evidence of bodies left in the tunnel before this whole business started. Take my hand. Now, before he kills him."

"I don't have enough strength," Laurel protested. "I might knock him down, but I don't think I can get Gabe out of here before he'll be after us again."

"I can help. So can the boys," Zoe panted.

"Just get it." Misty paused and gave Thickety a look. "What are you waiting for, demon? Now's your chance to gnaw on a soul. He's a ripe one, too."

Slowly, Laurel moved until the shovel was within reaching distance. She palmed it and clasped Misty's hand in hers. The ghost flickered into sight and as Gabe opened his eyes, Laurel was relieved to see a semblance of a smile flit across his features.

Saul moved in Misty's direction, intent to harm clearly on his face. "You. I killed you once for meddling in my affairs."

"Yeah. I'm here to return the favor." Misty shoved her sneakered foot against Laurel's and let the shovel swing with all of her might. The blow struck Saul in the face, knocking him back a few paces.

Randall and Lowell joined in, pulling

off the energy of Zoe and Laurel. As they faded into view, Saul's eyes widened.

"You bitch." He spit out blood and something that looked suspiciously like teeth. "I'm going to bury you where no one will ever find your body. Not. Ever." He charged Misty and Laurel, roaring obscenities as he flew.

Thickety roared his displeasure, his form twisting from the docile form of a cat to the demon he was. Shock and horror slid across Saul's face.

"What the fuck are you?"

"Death." Thickety smiled, his fangs white and gleaming in the faint light.

Saul screamed and tried to run as Thickety reached for him. "Now don't move. I believe these two ladies have a special gift just for you."

Zoe hobbled forward, and with her, so did the boys. They blocked Saul in when he tried to run.

"Not so fast," Zoe countered. "You just got here."

Laurel wrapped her arms around Misty's waist as she swung again, this time with the blade of the shovel. The snicking sound of the metal entering Saul's neck echoed in the dark tunnel.

Saul fell, gasping as bloody froth spilled from his lips into the cold dead earth.

EPILOGUE

"I DON'T KNOW. He looks kind of good with a cast on. Don't you think so, Nana?" Laurel grinned as she kissed Gabe on the cheek.

The new assisted living facility Laurel had moved her grandmother to was beyond perfect. The proceeds from the Greystone case would more than pay for Nana's stay for the rest of her life. Danvers had been horrified at what had transpired under his watch and had made it worth their time, and then some.

Saul's body had been dredged up and buried unceremoniously in an unmarked grave. He'd had no family to speak of; Laurel, Danvers, and Gabe had been the only ones to attend his funeral. Misty had flickered in for a minute, but watching the man who murdered her be put into the earth was the last thing she would wait around for.

"He does." Nana's eyes twinkled with merriment and then darted right back to the program she was watching on her new television. Jasper sat on the couch, completely transfixed by the moving pictures on the screen.

"You two," Gabe grumbled and crossed his arms across his chest, his lips twitching into a smile. He was healing nicely and had a very manly scar when she got him to take off his shirt. A cause she supported every possible chance she got.

"Hey. Don't forget me." Misty faded in, a superior look on her face. "You still owe me for that shovel work."

"That was some swing." Laurel grinned. "I'll have you on my team anytime."

"Good. A girl might get bored with nothing to do but float around all day. The afterlife is boring as hell." Misty craned around to see what Nana was watching. Eyes widening in delight, she perched on the edge of the couch.

"Ohhh. Now that's cool."

"What's cool?" Zoe hobbled from the

kitchen with a bowl of popcorn, each of her ghostly companions making sure she didn't teeter too much.

"This show. It's..."

"Wait! Is that..." Randall trilled, launching to an empty space on the couch, leaving Zoe to Lowell's tender mercies.

"Thank you all. I still can't believe all that has happened. What will become of Greystone?" Nana settled into her comfy chair, *Sharknado* playing on the DVR. "I love this channel. The sharks—"

"I knew it!" Randall crowed, his gaze glued to the screen in anticipation.

Thickety groaned. "Oh, man. Why do we have to watch this again?"

"Nobody asked you, cat." Nana reached for her iced tea and took a sip, smacking her lips in appreciation.

"I think Danvers is still planning on opening the park." Gabe scratched his chin, a grimace sliding over his face.

"After all that... wow." Misty grabbed for the TV guide but it slid right through her fingers. "Damn it. I wanted to see what was on tonight."

"So, you won't help us look over that haunted bookstore downtown? You would love it," Laurel teased.

Misty laughed. "I'm staying here. Nana has all the good shows. Ask me tomorrow." She flitted her fingers in a dismissive gesture. Her gaze, like Nana's, was plastered to the screen.

"Excuse us for a minute. I need to check to make sure I'm all packed." Laurel winked at Gabe and they got up to make room for Zoe and the boys.

Strolling to the guest room where Laurel had been staying until her Nana got settled, they shut the door and breathed a sigh of relief.

"Good move. I'm not a huge *Sharnado* fan." Gabe winced.

Laurel chuckled and tugged him down next to her on the bed. They sank down on the mattress and watched the retirees wander across the green with their golf clubs through the window.

Her grandmother was going to love it here.

"Well, that leaves us at loose ends, doesn't it?" Laurel snuggled in next to Gabe, careful not to touch his left shoulder. The lucky beads were wrapped around her wrist, proof that things would work out. She'd been dying to get a few minutes alone with him, but someone was always underfoot.

"It does."

"What do you say we get something to eat?" Laurel played with his hair. "Or maybe we could go and watch a movie. There's this new one called *Ghost House* I've been dying to see. Anything normal."

"Mmmm. Sounds good, but I had a different idea."

"Oh?"

"This." He captured her lips with his, leaning her back on the bed, wincing as he smacked his left shoulder and hissed his discomfort.

"Careful, they'll hear us." Laurel laughed.

"Let them. I've been trying to get you

alone since we got out of that place."

Laurel blinked, her lips turning up in a smile. "Lie down."

"What are you doing woman?"

"You'll see." She'd dressed with care this morning, making sure to leave her underwear safely in her drawer.

Straddling his lap, she toyed with the top button on his jeans.

"You have a wicked, wicked mind. I love it."

Laurel smiled and released his zipper, his erection springing free. "We only have a few minutes before they come looking for us."

Guiding him to her entrance, she sank down on his thick shaft. Sucking in her breath, she bit her lip and closed her eyes as the sensation of being stretched like never before rippled through her.

Hips moving, she rose and sank, crafting a rhythm that engulfed them both. Fire coursed through her blood as she climbed higher and higher, his shaft touching the deepest parts of her.

This was real.

No ghosts.

No phantoms.

Just him and her.

Gabe's fingers curled around the comforter, then strayed to her hips as she undulated, urging them both toward completion.

Fireworks sparked behind her eyes as he bucked beneath her and she had to clench her teeth from crying out and giving them away.

"Oh, God. I have to..." He flipped her

over, even though she knew the pain in his shoulder was going to make itself known fairly soon.

"Gabe..." She ran her fingers down the side of his face. He kept her tethered when she went beyond, and now, as her body soared to heights she'd never cared climb before.

Driving deep inside of her, he kissed her and buried his face in her hair, even as he thrust deep and hard. He gripped her hips and jerked, spilling inside of her as her own body spasmed around him.

He sank onto her, wincing, but the dreamy look in his so serious face was a gift all on its own. Gabe moved and rolled onto his back, pulling up his jeans, and flipping her skirt down.

"Well, I don't know about you, but I'd

really like to continue this at my place." He turned on his side and brushed his fingers alongside her face.

"I..." Laurel started to reply but the door burst open, a giggling Zoe holding hands with a very ghostly Lowell.

"Oh! Sorry. We thought this was the bathroom." Zoe bit her lip, a blush spreading over her cheeks.

"Looks like we all had the same idea for a minute of alone time." Laurel laughed, sitting up. "But good timing. A few seconds earlier and, well..."

"Oh my." Lowell laughed. "Well, I suppose we'll leave you to it and head back home."

"Don't leave on our account."

"We were just getting ready to pop over to my apartment." Gabe sat up, wrapping his good arm around Laurel.

"Thanks again, you guys. We couldn't have done this without you."

"It was our pleasure." Zoe gazed up at Lowell, her eyes filled with love.

"Truly."

"Well, come on. I want to show you my apartment, then we can talk about that new movie you wanted to see."

"Mmmm." Laurel kissed him on the cheek, reveling in the scrape of his five o'clock shadow over her lips, and then tugged her suitcase off the floor.

The whoops and hollers from the living room made her smile. This was their life and they were only getting started.

Thank you for reading.

Turn the page now for a preview from Blood Moon, Shadow Legacies Book Three. Coming soon to your favorite online retailer!

PREVIEW

MAGGIE BALDWIN STARED at her lifeless laptop and groaned. It wouldn't turn on. Again. So much for a lasting battery. Already irritated from lack of sleep, she pressed the on button one more time and tried to recall where she'd left the charger. It should have been in the little plastic bag she usually kept next to her laptop, but it wasn't.

It was too early for this. Even the

blaring television in the next room that she had on for company was getting on her nerves.

Goddess, but she needed coffee.

Stat.

The droning voice of the newscaster pushed onward, this time about police getting into an altercation with a suspect on the freeway and another so called peaceful protest gone sour with someone getting shot in the town square.

It was too much.

Life was already too stressful by far.

If she actually paid attention to the amount of crime that went on in this city, she would just get depressed. All that mattered now was the piece of crap machine in front of her and the deadline that was about to reach up and bite her in the ass.

Her fingers tingled and she stuffed her wild magic down. It would be easy to locate the charger by magic, but then she would pay for the stupid waste of power before breakfast for the rest of the day with a migraine and little to nothing in the way of progress on her pages.

"Stupid computer. I can't believe this. I ought to just replace you and be done with it."

She growled and pushed herself up from the small space at the kitchen table. Perhaps it was in her work bag in the foyer. Resorting to magic when real world solutions worked just fine had proven to be more of a hindrance than a help. At least for her.

Her wobbly magic had been a point of

contention with her mother for years. She wasn't very good at it. Wish for rain and get a flood in her kitchen. That was her world right now. It was just better to accept what was real and get on with her life.

Like with her marriage.

It was over, and no amount of wishing and hoping was going to fix it.

With what she'd found out with just a couple of calls to a private investigator, it was the mayo on a shit sandwich.

Maggie sighed and peered into the bag.

Nothing.

"Oh. This just keeps getting better and better."

Spinning on her heel, Maggie nibbled on her lip and considered her next move.

She had a deadline for her publisher, and today would be her only day off with no distractions until next week. Not that she could focus, anyway.

The divorce papers were on her desk. She had every intention of serving them, especially after the private investigator found the porn on his computer and narrowed down the missing money from their bank account.

At first, she'd assumed she'd made an accounting error with last month's bills. But that hadn't been it at all.

Hotels.

And trips to a detail car wash off the freeway.

He'd supposedly been out with the boys from the club, but something in the back of her mind kept digging at her.

Their poker games didn't last that long. Neither did their dinners at the club, which she now refused to attend. Not after the last time with his uppity friends and their equally unpleasant wives. She didn't fit in with the country club scene, and that was more than all right with her.

Scott hadn't come home—again—by the time her head hit the pillow last night a little after midnight. It was becoming par for the course. Maggie couldn't concentrate on anything, and that included leaving her damn charging cable someplace. She could swear it was next to her workstation last night when she went to bed, but she could have been dreaming. She couldn't remember, and that just pissed her off, making her already foul mood even more noxious.

Seeing things that weren't there had begun to be a habit and she didn't like it one bit. A blink and whatever it was vanished, but it was becoming more and more the norm.

Maybe she was working too much. Deadlines always did make her a little bit hard boiled. Add in the crap with Scott and she was starting to feel like an egg salad.

Two nights ago, she had fallen asleep after a long day at the shop and writing, and he woke her in the middle of the night, demanding she do the laundry.

An acerbic comment had been poised on the tip of her tongue, but then she noticed the blood on his shirt. Something inside her prickled to attention and she squashed it down, trying to focus on Scott.

"What happened?" She'd blurted out, startled by the abrupt way he'd shaken her awake.

Then, she saw the hazy outline of something hovering in the doorway behind him.

Holy shit.

The old Scott would have apologized for waking her. But this man who stood in front of her made the flesh on her arms crawl and the dark sensation inside her rouse just a little bit more.

No.

She tamped it down again, determined not to let it out, just as she had when she was a kid.

Blood magic was wrong.

But why did it keep cropping up in her life?

And who the fuck was standing in her bedroom door?

She didn't want to wait around to find out. The other shadows at the edge of her vision had always shied away when she trained her gaze on them. This one did not. She stared at Maggie with terror in her eyes and her lips moved, as if she were trying to speak but nothing was coming out.

That was enough to motivate her into action. She'd never been afraid of her husband before that moment, but when her questions were met with stone cold silence, she felt the chasm between them widen irreparably. There was nothing even resembling the man she married behind his eyes, and everything in her told her to run.

What had he been doing out there in the dark?

The energy around him swirled and snapped with menace and she wished for all she was worth that she had at least a modicum of her mother's earth magic within her.

She grabbed his shirt and fled to the laundry room, slamming the door and locking it behind her, alternatively drawn and repelled by the shirt in her grasp.

He never said a word, but she felt his eyes boring into her every step.

Her skin crawled and the shirt in her hands felt alive with residual energy.

Goddess bless.

What had he done?

And what had he awakened in her?

Her mother warned her to never allow him see her magic and she never understood why. But the darkness in his eyes tonight drew the memory back like a slap to the face.

Had her mother been trying to keep her talent stifled, or had she been attempting to protect her?

Tears swam in her eyes and she angrily dashed them away.

Now was not the time to let the past haunt her. She had some very real problems and she had to have a clear head to think.

There was no other way around it. She was going to have to go to the shop and stay there until everything boiled over. Living here and trying to work things out was ludicrous. Especially with what she knew. He'd been lying to her for months. She just hadn't seen it coming.

Correction... she hadn't wanted to. Because then her mother would have been right. Scott loved her.

Didn't he?

Hell, she was standing here holding a bloody shirt, and the man didn't look like he had a mark on him.

And she was afraid.

Not to mention her unwanted houseguests.

"The blood." She stared at the shirt, in turn drawn by the violence of the splatter and repulsed at the same time.

A hum began in her veins, the magic

inside of her unfurling like a poisonous flower.

Blood.

Dark.

Dangerous.

Seductive.

Blood.

When she touched the gore, images of pain and terror flooded her mind's eye. Over and over, she watched a woman screaming as a knife slashed at her prone body.

Plastic sheeting coated in blood.

A single lightbulb swinging in the darkness and a small window looking out into *her back yard.*

"Ohhhhh."

Maggie clutched her stomach as acid rushed up the back of her throat. That was her kitchen window. Her herb garden.

No.

Oh... oh, my Goddess.

What was this?

What had she seen?

Then it hit her. The woman standing behind her husband was the person she'd perceived in the vision.

Who was she?

Well, other than a ghost in her bedroom, that is.

Feeling for her phone, she had a moment of panic when she realized it was still on the charger on the nightstand next to the bed.

The tears started and wouldn't stop. Maggie slumped on the floor and threw the shirt away from her. She searched the plastic bins against the wall and located a random screwdriver. Clutching it in her hands, she hunkered down and eyed the locked door.

The knob hadn't moved. She would have heard it.

Everything with the detective agency had been online, with a new email Scott knew nothing about. She'd password protected her laptop and phone.

She couldn't wash it. Not now, not after she'd seen the things she'd seen.

You could see more.

The voice whispered to her, the old urges of the blood magic she'd tried as a kid in rebellion against her mother. Instead of listening, she put her hands over her ears and tried to fight it.

Soon, tears and exhaustion took over

and she let the darkness take her into cool oblivion.

When she came to, she found herself sprawled out on the floor, her face pressed against the tile, cheeks coated with tears.

Fear was a cold stone in the bottom of her stomach.

The blood was not her husband's. Nowhere in the database search, did the detective agency find something criminal, or they would have called her in for a face-to-face meeting.

But now, she knew the truth.

Instead of washing the shirt, she tucked it into an old grocery bag and buried it beneath the washer in the compartment that held household towels and cleaning rags. He would never look there. If he asked about the shirt, she could tell him it got ruined at the wash.

Did he know about the divorce papers?

The thought filled her with dread.

The first thing she needed to do was call the detective agency and let them know what happened.

She wiped her hands on her nightgown and took a deep breath, the events of last night flooding through her mind.

She had no idea what time it was.

Goddess, was he still here?

Craning her head against the window, she eyed the driveway. Scott's car was gone. That meant it was after eight.

Okay.

Releasing the breath she'd forgotten she was holding, Maggie drooped against the wall.

Her hand fumbled with the lock on the laundry room door and she stumbled out into the kitchen.

She poured the water into the coffeepot with shaking hands and flipped on the switch, sighing as the rich aroma of the Columbian blend pervaded the kitchen.

It was just after eight, according to the clock on the stove. But she had survived the night.

Nightmares of him coming into the bedroom filled her dreams, but this time, the blood on his shirt was hers.

Shaking it off, she wandered into the other room as the coffee percolated.

A quick check of the papers on her desk didn't reveal whether he knew about the papers or not. He must have left sometime after she'd locked herself into the laundry room.

That was fine. It would give her time to think of what to do.

The apartment above the shop hadn't been used since her mother, but it would do for now. No way was she going to spend another night under this roof.

The images of the woman staring back at her made her shiver, and she realized she hadn't seen anything out of the corner of her eye since she'd woken.

She hadn't seen anything during the day, now that she thought about it.

A knock sounded on the door and she paused mid action.

Who could that be so early?

Annoyance that it was a salesman slid through her veins. So did fear. Home invasions were on the rise with all the political unrest.

But would they knock first?

She wasn't sure.

That was another point of contention with her husband. Their home security system and outdoor cameras had stopped working years ago and he'd refused to have it fixed.

Every time she brought it up, he'd countered her.

Now, she wished she'd just gone ahead and had the repair guy come out anyway. At least then she wouldn't feel so alone.

Nibbling on her lip, she padded to the

front door and tried to make out a face through the leaded glass.

Nothing.

Sneaking a peek through the side window, she found a uniformed officer standing there.

Relief warred with concern, her heartbeat loud in her ears.

Mystified, she opened the door.

"Can I help you, officer?"

"Ma'am. We have some unfortunate news. Your husband is dead."

Dear Reader,

Thank you for reading *Ghost Moon, Shadow Legacies Book Two.* If you enjoyed the book, please consider leaving a review on the retailer website where you made your purchase.

If you would like more information about my other titles or would like to sign up for my newsletter and receive a free copy of Map of Bones, please follow the link:

http://erzabetwrites.wix.com/erzabet bishop

All the very best to you and yours,

XOXO

Erzabet Bishop

WHERE TO FIND MORE

OF ERZABET BISHOP

Twitter

@erzabetbishop

Instagram

https://www.instagram.com/erzabetbis

hop/

Bookbub

https://www.bookbub.com/authors/erz

abet-bishop

Website and Newsletter

http://erzabetwrites.wix.com/erzabetbi
shop

Facebook Author Page
https://www.facebook.com/erzabetbish
opauthor

Goodreads
http://www.goodreads.com/author/sho
w/6590718.Erzabet_Bishop

Street team
https://www.facebook.com/groups/101
8269998190112/

ALSO BY ERZABET BISHOP

Silver Circle Witches Series

Red Moon Rising

Blue Moon Rising

Harvest Moon Rising

Blood Moon Rising

Speed Dating with the Denizens of the Underworld Series

Lucifer

Demi

Hera

GHOST MOON

Medusa

Artemis

Shadow Legacies Series

Hunter Moon

Ghost Moon

Blood Moon

Coming Soon!

Born of Hellfire Series

Hellbound Heart

Demon's Playground

Devil's Mate

Shifting Hearts Dating Agency Series

Hedging Her Bets

Waking Up Wolf

ERZABET BISHOP & GINA KINCADE

Kitten Around

Shifting Hearts Dating Agency Collection
Books 1-3

Shifting Hearts Dating App Series

Mistle Tie Me

Your Wolfish Heart

Chocolate Moon Cafe

Bear It All

Outfoxing Her Mate

Shifting Hearts Dating App: Books 1-3

My Wicked Mates Series

Craving Her Mates

Surrendering to Her Mate

Tormenting Her Mate

My Wicked Mates   Series Collection:

GHOST MOON

Books 1-3

Westmore Wolves Series

Wicked for You

Heart's Protector

Burning for You

Taming the Beast

Mistletoe Kisses

Westmore Wolves Collection, Books 1-5

Curse Workers Series

Sanguine Shadows

Map of Bones

Malediction

Arcane

ERZABET BISHOP & GINA KINCADE

Curse Workers Collection: Books 1-3

Sigil Fire Series

Sigil Fire

Written on Skin

Glitter Lust

First Christmas: A Sigil Fire Holiday Romance

Sigil Fire Books 1-3: An Urban Fantasy Boxed Set

Collections and Anthologies

Holidays and More:

A Lesfic Short Story Collection

Lesfic Tales:

A Lesfic Short Story Collection

GHOST MOON

Sapphic Holiday Cruise:

A Lesbian Holiday Collection

Sweet Sensations:

A Short Story Anthology

Standalone Novels

Snow

ABOUT ERZABET BISHOP

ERZABET BISHOP IS A USA TODAY BESTSELLING and award-winning author of over forty paranormal and contemporary romance books. She lives in Houston, Texas, and when she isn't writing about sexy shifters or voluptuous heroines, she enjoys playing in local bookstores and watching movies with her husband and furry kids.

MORE FROM GINA KINCADE

Silver Circle Witches

Red Moon Rising

Blue Moon Rising

Harvest Moon Rising

Blood Moon Rising

Speed Dating with the Denizens of the Underworld

Lucifer

Demi

GHOST MOON

Hera

Medusa

Artemis

Shadow Legacies

Hunter Moon

Ghost Moon

Blood Moon

Coming Soon!

Born of Hellfire

Hellbound Heart

Demon's Playground

Devil's Mate

Shifting Hearts Dating App

Mistle Tie Me

Bear It All

Chocolate Moon Cafe

ERZABET BISHOP & GINA KINCADE

Your Wolfish Heart

Outfoxing Her Mate

Shifting Hearts Dating App: Books 1-3

Shifting Hearts Dating Agency

One True Mate: Furever Shifter Mates,
Book 2

Green Rock Falls

Accidentally Forever

CONNECT WITH GINA

Facebook

https://www.facebook.com/authorgina

kincade

Newsletter Mailing List

https://landing.mailerlite.com/webform

s/landing/r1r5n4

Amazon

https://www.amazon.com/Gina-

Kincade/e/B00WSRLHVO/

Twitter

https://twitter.com/ginakincade

GHOST MOON

BookBub

https://www.bookbub.com/authors/gina-kincade

Blog/Webpage:

https://www.ginakincade.com

Instagram

https://www.instagram.com/ginakincade

Goodreads

https://www.goodreads.com/ginakincade

ABOUT GINA KINCADE

USA Today Bestselling Author Gina Kincade spends her days tapping away at a keyboard, through blood, sweat, and often many tears, crafting steamy paranormal romances filled with shifters and vampires, along with witchy urban fantasy tales in magical worlds she hopes her readers yearn to crawl into.

A busy mom of three, she loves healthy home cooking, gardening, warm beaches, fast cars, and horseback riding.

Ms. Kincade's life is full, time is never on her side, and she wouldn't change a moment of it!

Find more from Gina at:
https://www.ginakincade.com/

CPSIA information can be obtained
at www.ICGtesting.com
Printed in the USA
BVHW052122140223
658501BV00012B/212